Robert Anderson

The Life of Samuel Johnson

Robert Anderson

The Life of Samuel Johnson

ISBN/EAN: 9783337333669

Printed in Europe, USA, Canada, Australia, Japan

Cover: Foto ©Raphael Reischuk / pixelio.de

More available books at **www.hansebooks.com**

THE

LIFE

OF

SAMUEL JOHNSON, LL. D.

WITH

CRITICAL OBSERVATIONS

ON HIS WORKS.

BY ROBERT ANDERSON, M. D.

LONDON:

PRINTED FOR J. & A. ARCH; AND FOR BELL & BRADFUTE,
AND J. MUNDELL & CO. EDINBURGH.

1795.

THE LIFE

OF

JOHNSON.

THE events of the life of JOHNSON, " the brighteſt ornament of the eighteenth century," who has written the lives of ſo many eminent perſons, and ſo much enriched our national ſtock of criticiſm and biography, have been related by friend and foe, by panegyriſts and ſatirical defamers, by the lovers of anecdote, and the followers of party, with a diligence of reſearch, a minuteneſs of detail, a variety of illuſtration, and a felicity of deſcription, unexampled in the records of literary biography.

Befides feveral flight fketches of his life, by unknown authors, taken, fometimes with a favourable, flattering pencil, fome- times in the broader ftyle of caricature, which lie fcattered in the periodical pu- blications of the laft ten years; volumin- ous biographical accounts of him have been given to the world by Thomas Tyers, Efq. Mrs. Piozzi, Dr. Towers, Sir John Hawkins, James Bofwell, Efq. and Arthur Murphy, Efq. who were his moft intimate friends, and wrote from perfonal know- ledge. Their feveral publications, which place his character in very different, and often oppofite points of light, by exhibit- ing a ftriking likenefs of the features of his mind, which were ftrong and promi- nent, and by recording fo confiderable a portion of his wifdom and wit, have ex- quifitely gratified the lovers of literary anecdotes, and largely contributed to the inftruction and entertainment of mankind. The publications of Mr. Tyers, Mrs. Piozzi, Dr. Towers, and Mr. Murphy, come under the defcription of "Biographical Sketches," "Anecdotes," and "Effays." Thofe of Sir John Hawkins and Mr. Bofwell are more elaborately compofed, and entitle them to the exclufive appellation of his biographers.

On an attentive perufal, it will be found that the narrative of Sir John Hawkins contains a collection of curious anecdotes and obfervations, which few men but its author could have brought together; but a very fmall part of it relates to the perfon who is the fubject of the work. He appears to be a worthy, and often a well-informed man, but he poffeffes neither animation nor correctnefs, expanfion of intellect, nor elegance of tafte. He writes without much feeling or fentiment; his work is heavy, cold, and prolix; but we difcover in it many gleams of good fenfe, and openings of humanity, fometimes checked by ignorance, and fometimes by prejudice.

The narrative of Mr. Bofwell is written with more comprehenfion of mind, accuracy of intelligence, clearnefs of narration, and elegance of language; and is more ftrongly marked by the *defiderium chari capitis*, which is the firft feature of affectionate remembrance. He was peculiarly fitted for the tafk of recording the fayings and actions of this extraordinary man, by his affiduous attention. From the commencement of his acquaintance with him in 1763, he had the fcheme of writing his life conftantly in view; and continued his collections, with his approbation and affiftance, with unwearied diligence, and meritorious perféverance, for upwards of twenty years. He gave a fpecimen of his being able to preferve his converfation, in an authentic and lively manner, in his " Journal of a Tour to the Hebrides," 8vo, 1786. His veneration and efteem for his friend, induced him, at a fubfequent period, to go through the laborious tafk of digefting and arranging the immenfe mafs of materials, which his own diligence, and the kindnefs of others, had furnifhed him, and of forming the hiftory of his life ; which was publifhed in 2 vols. 4to, 1791, and was received by the world with moft extraordinary avidity.

Xenophon's *Memorabilia* of Socrates may poffibly have fuggefted to Mr. Bofwell the idea of preferving and giving to the world the *Memorabilia* of his venerable friend ; but he profeffes to have followed the model of Mafon in his " Memoirs of Gray." He has, however, the advantage of Mafon, in the quantity, variety, and richnefs of his materials. His work may be referred to that clafs of compilements known by the name of " Books in *Ana*." To compare it with Monnoye's edition of the *Me-nagiana*, one of the moſt eſteemed of theſe publications, would not be doing juſtice to it. The incidental *converſations* between ſo eminent an inſtructor of mankind, and his friends, the numerous body of *anecdotes*, literary and biographical, and the *letters* which are occaſionally interſperſed, and naturally introduced, in the narrative part of Mr. Boſwell's ample performance, open and diſcloſe to the eager curioſity of rational and laudable inquiry, an immenſe ſtorehouſe of mental treaſure, which far exceeds, in merit and value, the voluminous collections of the wiſe and witty ſayings of the learned and ingenious men of other nations. With ſome venial exceptions on the ſcore of egotiſm and indiſcriminate admiration, his work exhibits the moſt copious, intereſting, and finiſhed picture of the life and opinions of an eminent man, that was ever executed; and is juſtly eſteemed one of the moſt inſtructive and entertaining books in the Engliſh language.

The eccentricities of Mr. Boſwell, it is uſeleſs to detail. They have already been the ſubject of ridicule in various different forms and publications, by men of ſuperficial underſtanding, and ludicrous fancy. Many have ſuppoſed him to be a mere relater of the ſayings of others; but he poſſeſſed conſiderable intellectual powers, for which he has not had ſufficient credit. It is manifeſt to every reader of any diſcernment, that he could never have collected ſuch a maſs of information, and juſt obſervations on human life, as his very valuable work contains, without great ſtrength of mind, and much various knowledge; as he never could have diſplayed his collections in ſo lively a manner, had he not poſſeſſed a very pictureſque imagination, or, in other words, had he not had a very happy turn for poetry, as well as for humour and for wit.

This lively and ingenious biographer, is now beyond the reach of praife or cenfure. He died at London, May 19, 1795, in the 55th year of his age. His death is an irreparable lofs to Englifh literature. He had many failings; and many virtues, and many amiable qualities, which predominated over the frailties incident to human nature. He will be long regretted by a wide circle of friends, to whom his good qualities and focial talents always made his company a valuable acceffion.

The facts ftated in the prefent account are chiefly taken from the narratives of Sir John Hawkins, and Mr. Bofwell; with the addition of fuch particulars of the progrefs of his mind and fortunes, as the fubfequent narrative of Mr. Murphy, and the moft refpectable periodical publications of the laft ten years have fupplied.

[9]

SAMUEL JOHNSON was born at Litchfield, in Staffordshire, September 7. 1709. His father, Michael Johnson, was a native of Cubley, in Derbyshire, of obscure extraction, who settled in Litchfield as a bookseller, and carried on that business at all the neighbouring towns on market days; but was so respectable as to be made one of the magistrates of that city. He was a man of a large and robust body, and of a strong and active mind; but was always subject to a morbid melancholy. He was a zealous high-church-man and Jacobite; though he reconciled himself by casuistical arguments of expediency and necessity, to take the oaths imposed by the prevailing power. He was a pretty good Latin scholar, and being a man of good sense and skill in his trade, he acquired a reasonable share of wealth, of which he afterwards lost the greatest part, by engaging, unsuccessfully, in the manufacture of parchment. His mother, Sarah Ford, defcended of an ancient race of fubftantial yeomanry in Warwickfhire, was the fifter of Dr. Jofeph Ford, a phyfician of confiderable eminence, and father of the famous Cornelius Ford, Chaplain to Lord Chefterfield, fuppofed to be the Parfon in Hogarth's " Modern Midnight Converfation," a man of great parts, but of very profligate manners. She was a woman of diftinguifhed underftanding, prudence, and piety. They were well advanced in years when they married, and had only another child, named Nathaniel, who feems to have fucceeded his father in his bufinefs; but died in 1737, in the 25th year of his age.

During the period of infancy, all children are prodigies of form and underftanding to their parents. With a natural fondnefs, they exaggerate every fymptom of fenfe into the perfection of wifdom, and defcribe every feature with an adventitious grace. If the object of their admiration fhould at more mature years become diftinguifhed for excellence, it is hoped that we may believe wonders of the child, becaufe we have feen greatnefs in the man. Hence, in our fondnefs for the marvellous, the traditions of the nurfery, refpecting fuch perfons, are amplified beyond the bounds of credibility, and recited with all the confidence of truth.

Every great genius muft begin with a prodigy; and it is not to be fuppofed that Johnfon fhould be without atteftations of thefe miracles of early genius, which are believed by fome to be as neceffary to the attainment of future pre-eminence, as that fruits fhould be preceded by the bloffom. Among other ftories of his infant precocity generally circulated, and generally believed, we are told by Mrs. Piozzi, and Sir

John Hawkins, that, at the age of three years, he trod by accident upon one of a brood of eleven ducks, and killed it, and upon that occasion made the following verses:

> Here lies good master duck,
>   Whom Samuel Johnson trod on;
> If it had liv'd, it had been *good luck*,
> For then we'd had an *odd one*.

This prodigy is scarcely exceeded by the bees on Plato's lips, or the doves that covered the infant poet with leaves and flowers; for how should a child of three years old make regular verses, and in alternate rhyme? The internal evidence is sufficient to counterbalance any testimony that these verses could be the production of a child of such an early age. But, fortunately, credulity is relieved from the burden of doubt, by Johnson's having himself assured Mr. Boswell, that they were made by his father, who wished them to pass for his fon's. He added, " my father was a foolifh old man, that is to fay, foolifh in talking of his children."

He derived from his parents, or from an unwholefome nurfe, the diftemper called the King's Evil. Jacobites at that time believed in the efficacy of the royal touch. His mother, yielding to this fuperftitious notion, in her anxiety for his cure, when he was two years old (by the advice of Sir John Floyer, then a phyfician at Litchfield), carried him to London, where he was actually touched by Queen Anne. But the difeafe, too obftinate to yield to remedies more powerful, greatly disfigured his countenance, naturally harfh and rugged, impaired his hearing, and deprived him of the fight of his left eye.

He was firft taught to read Englifh by Dame Oliver, a widow, who kept a fchool for young children in Litchfield. His next inftructor, in Englifh, was a mafter whom he familiarly called Tom Brown, who he said " publifhed a fpelling-book, and dedicated it to the Universe." He began to learn Latin in the free-fchool of Litchfield, at firft under the care of Mr. Hawkins, the under-mafter, whom he has defcribed as " a man fkilful in his little way." In about two years, he rofe to be under the tuition of Mr. Hunter, the head-mafter, a very refpectable teacher, and a worthy man; but who, according to his account, was " very fevere, and wrong headedly fevere." He had for his fchool-fellows Dr. James, inventor of the fever-powder, Mr. Lowe, canon of Windfor, Dr. Taylor, rector of Afhbourne, and Mr. Hector, furgeon in Birmingham, with whom he contracted a particular intimacy.

While at fchool, he is faid by Mr. Hector to have been indolent and averfe from ftudy. But the procraftination of his duties feems neither to have prevented the

timely performance·of his exercifes, nor
to have blemifhed them with inaccuracies;
for " he was never known to have been
corrected at fchool, unlefs for talking and
diverting other boys from their bufinefs."
Indeed, fuch was the fuperiority of his talents above thofe of his companions, that
three of the boys, of whom Mr. Hector
was fometimes one, are faid to have affembled fubmiffively every morning, to carry
him triumphantly upon their fhoulders to
fchool. This ovation is believed by Mr.
Bofwell to have been an honour paid to
the early predominance of his intellectual
powers alone; but they who remember
what boys are, and who confider that
Johnfon's corporeal prowefs was by no
means defpicable, will be apt to fufpect
that the homage was enforced, at leaft as
much by awe of the one, as by admiration of the other.

After having refided for fome months at the houfe of his coufin, Cornelius Ford, who affifted him in the claffics, he was, by his advice, at the age of fifteen, removed to the fchool of Stourbridge in Worcester-fhire, of which Mr. Wentworth was then mafter, whom he has defcribed as " a very able man, but an idle man, and to me un-reafonably fevere. Yet he taught me a great deal." He feems to have been there in the double capacity of a fcholar and ufh-er, repaying the learning he acquired from his mafter, by the inftruction he gave to the younger boys. Parfon Ford he has defcribed in his " Life of Fenton," as " a clergyman at that time too well known, whofe abilities, inftead of furnifhing con-vivial merriment to the voluptuous and the diffolute, might have enabled him to excel among the virtuous and the wife."

He thus difcriminated to Dr. Percy, Bifhop of Dromore, his progrefs at his two grammar-fchools: " At one I learnt much in the fchool, but little from the mafter; in the other I learnt much from the mafter, but little in the fchool."

He remained at Stourbridge little more than a year, and then returned home, where he purfued his ftudies; but not upon any regular plan. Of this method of attaining knowledge, he feems ever after to have entertained a favourable opinion, and to have recommended it, not without reafon, to young men, as the fureft means of enticing them to learn. What he read was not works of mere amufement. " They were not voyages and travels, but all literature, all ancient authors, all manly; though but little Greek, only fome of Anacreon and Hefiod. But in this irregular manner, I had looked into a great many books, which were not commonly known at the univerfities, where they feldom read any books but what are put into their hands by their tutors; fo that when I came to Oxford, Dr. Adams told me I was the beft qualified for the univerfity that he had ever known come there."

He had already given feveral proofs of his poetical genius, both in his fchool exercifes, and in other occafional compofitions. Of thefe Mr. Bofwell obtained a confiderable collection from Mr. Wentworth, the fon of his mafter, and Mr. Hector, his fchool-fellow; of which he has preferved fome tranflations from *Homer*, *Virgil*, *Horace*, &c. Unfortunately the communications of Mr. Wentworth are not diftinguifhed from thofe of Mr. Hector. Such a precaution would have enabled us to have diftinguifhed with certainty the efforts of the boy, from the production of riper years. His tranflation of the *firft eclogue of Virgil*, is not fo harmonious as that from the *fixth book of Homer*; and both are inferior in this refpect to thofe which he has made of the *Odes of Horace*. Indeed, in the ftyle and manner of verfification ufed in the laft; and in fome other of his juvenile pieces, he feems to have made little alteration in his more experienced days; and it muft be added, that in point of fmoothnefs, little improvement could have been made.

After a refidence of two years at home, Mr. Andrew Corbet, a gentleman of Shropfhire, undertook to fupport him at Oxford, in the character of a companion to his fon, one of his fchool-fellows, " though, in fact," fays Mr. Bofwell, upon the authority of Dr. Taylor, " he never received any affiftance whatever from that gentleman." He was accordingly entered a Commoner at Pembroke College, Oxford, October 31: 1728, being then in his nineteenth year.

On the night of his arrival at Oxford, his father, who had anxioufly accompa-

nied him, found means to have him introduced to Mr. Jorden, Fellow of Pembroke,
who was to be his tutor. According to
Dr. Adams, who was prefent, he feemed
very full of the merits of his fon, and told
the company he was a good fcholar and a
poet, and wrote Latin verfes. His figure
and manner feemed ftrange to them; but
he behaved modeftly, and fat filent, till,
upon fomething which occurred in the
courfe of converfation, he fuddenly ftruck
in, and quoted Macrobius; and this gave
the firft impreffion of that extenfive reading in which he had indulged himfelf.

Of his tutor, Mr. Jorden, he gave Mr.
Bofwell the following account: " He was
a very worthy man, but a heavy man, and
I did not profit much by his inftruction.
Indeed, I did not attend him much." He
had, however, a love and refpect for Jorden, not for his literature, but for his
worth. " Whenever (faid he) a young

man becomes Jorden's pupil, he becomes his fon."

The fifth of November was at that time kept with great folemnity at Pembroke College, and exercifes upon the gunpowder plot were required. Johnfon neglected to perform his. To apologize for his neglect, he gave in a fhort copy of verfes, intituled *Somnium*, containing a common thought, " that the mufe had come to him in his fleep, and whifpered that it did not become him to write on fuch fubjects as politics ; he fhould confine himfelf to humbler themes ;" but the verfification was truly Virgilian.

Having given fuch a fpecimen of his poetical powers, he was afked by Mr. Jorden to tranflate Pope's *Meffiah* into Latin hexameter verfe, as a Chriftmas exercife. He performed it with uncommon rapidity, and in fo mafterly a manner, that he obtained great applaufe from it, which ever after kept him high in the estimation of his college and indeed of all the university. Pope, impelled by gratitude and taste, perhaps not unassisted by vanity, is reported to have said concerning it, " that the author would leave it a question for posterity, whether his or mine be the original?" It was first printed by his father, without his knowledge; and afterwards inserted in a " Miscellany," published by subscription at Oxford, in 1731, by Mr. John Husbands, Fellow of Pembroke College.

The particular course of his reading while at Oxford, and during the time of vacation which he passed at home, cannot be traced. From his earliest years he loved to read poetry and romances of chivalry. He read Shakspeare at a period so early, that the speech of the ghost in " Hamlet" terrified him when he was alone. Horace's odes were the compositions he moft liked in early life ; but it was long before he could relifh his fatires and epiftles. He told Mr. Bofwell, what he read *folidly* at Oxford was Greek, not the Grecian hiftorians, but Homer and Euripides, and now and then a little epigram ; that the ftudy of which he was moft fond was metaphyfics ; but he had not read much even in that way. We may be abfolutely certain, however, both from his writings and his converfation, that his reading was very extenfive. He projected a common-place book to the extent of fix folio volumes, but according to Sir John Hawkins, the blank leaves far exceeded the written ones.

In 1729, while at Litchfield, during the college vacation, the " morbid melancholy" which was lurking in his conftitution, gathered fuch ftrength as to afflict him in a dreadful manner. He was overwhelmed with an horrible hypocondria, with perpetual irritation, fretfulnefs, and impatience, and with a dejection, gloom, and defpair, that made exiftence mifery. He fancied himfelf feized by, or approaching to in-fanity; in conformity with which notion he applied, when he was at the very worft, to his godfather, Dr. Swinfen, phyfician in Litchfield, and put into his hand a ftate of his cafe, written in Latin; " which fhowed," as Mr. Bofwell expreffes it, " an uncommon vigour, not only of fancy and tafte, but of judgment." That he fhould have fuppofed himfelf approach-ing to infanity, at the very time when he was giving proofs of a more than ordinary foundnefs and vigour of judgment, is lefs ftrange than that Mr. Bofwell fhould confider the vigour of *fancy*, which he dif-played on fuch a fubject, a proof of his fa-nity. It is a common effect of melancholy to make thofe who are afflicted with it imagine that they are actually fuffering

thofe evils which happen to be moft
ftrongly prefented to their minds. But
there is a clear diftinction between a diforder which affects only the imagination
and fpirits, while the judgment is found,
and a diforder by which the judgment itfelf is impaired. Whatever be the arguments in favour of free-will, of volition
unreftrained by the force and prevalence
of motives, it muft be allowed that the
effects of reafon on the human mind are
not at all times, and on all fubjects, equally powerful. The mind, like the body,
has its weak organs; in other words, the
impreffions on fome fubjects are fo deeply
fixed, that the judgment is no longer able
to guide the operations of the mind, in
reafoning on, or in judging of them. The
imagination feizes the rein, and till the
force of the idea is leffened from habit,
the ufual powers are fufpended. But this
is not madnefs; for ftrong impreffions of

various kinds, will, in different minds, produce fimilar effects. From this difmal malady, which he " did not then know how
to manage," he never afterwards was perfectly relieved; and all his labours, and all
his employments, were but temporary in-
terruptions of its baleful influence.

In the hiftory of his mind, his religious
progrefs is an important article. He had
been early inftructed in the doctrines of the
church of England, by his mother, who continued her pious care with affiduity, but in
his opinion, not with judgment. "Sunday"
faid he " was a heavy day to me when I
was a boy. My mother confined me on
Sundays, and made me read " The Whole
Duty of Man," from a great part of which
I could derive no inftruction. When, for
inftance, I read the chapter on theft, which,
from infancy, I had been taught was wrong,
I was no more convinced that theft was
wrong than before; fo there was no accef-

fion of knowledge. A boy fhould be introduced to fuch books by having his attention directed to the arrangement, to the
ftyle, and other excellencies of compofition, that the mind being thus engaged by
an amufing variety of objects, may not
grow weary."

' He communicated to Mr. Bofwell the
following account of " the firft occafion of
his thinking in earneft of religion." I fell
into an inattention to religion, or an indifference about it, in my ninth year. The
church at Litchfield, in which we had a
feat, wanted reparation: fo I was to go
and find a feat in other churches; and
having bad eyes, and being awkward a-
bout this, I ufed to go and read in the
fields on Sunday. This habit continued
till my fourteenth year, and ftill I find a
great reluctance to go to church. I then
became a fort of lax *talker* againft religion,
for I did not much *think* about it; and

this lafted till I went to Oxford, where it would not be *fuffered*. When at Oxford, I took up Law's " Serious Call to the Un-converted," expecting to find it a dull book (as fuch books generally are), and perhaps to laugh at it. But I found Law quite an over-match for me ; and this was the firft occafion of my thinking in ear-neft of religion, after I became capable of rational inquiry."

Serious impreffions of religion, from particular incidents, it is certain, have been experienced by many pious perfons ; though it muft be acknowledged, that weak minds, from an erroneous fuppofition, that no man is in a ftate of grace, who has not felt a particular converfion, have, in fome cafes, brought a degree of ridicule upon them ; a ridicule of which it is inconfide-rate or unfair to make a general applica-tion. How ferioufly Johnfon was impref-fed with a fenfe of religion, from this time forward, appears from the whole tenor of his life and writings. Religion was the predominant object of his thoughts; though he feems not to have attained all the tranquillity and affurance in his practice of its duties that are fo earneftly to be defired. His fentiments, upon points of abftract virtue and rectitude, were in the higheft degree elevated and generous, but he was unfortunate enough to have the fublimity of his mind degraded by the hypochondriacal propenfities of his animal conftitution. The ferenity, the independence, and the exultation of religion, were fentiments to which he was a ftranger. He faw the Almighty in a different light from what he is reprefented in the purer page of the gofpel; and he trembled in the prefence of Infinite Goodnefs. Thofe tenets of the church of England, which are moft nearly allied to Calvinifm, were congenial to his general feelings, and they made an early impreffion, which habits confirmed, and which reafon, if ever exerted, could not efface. At the latter part of his life thefe terrors had a confiderable effect; nor was their influence loft, till difeafe had weakened his powers, and blunted his feelings.

The year following, 1730, Mr Corbet left the univerfity, and his father, to whom, according to Sir John Hawkins, he trufted for fupport, declined contributing any farther to Johnfon's maintenance, than paying for his Commons. His father's bufinefs was by no means lucrative. His remittances, confequently, were too fmall even to fupply the decencies of external appearance; and the very fhoes that he wore were fo much torn, that they could no longer conceal his feet. So jealous, however, was he of appearing an object of eleemofynary contribution, that a new pair having been placed at his door, by

fome unknown hand, he flung them a-
way with indignation.

While thus oppreffed by want, he feems
to have yielded to that indifference to
fame and improvement, which is the off-
fpring of defpair. "He was generally
feen," fays Dr. Percy, "lounging at the
college gate, with a circle of young ftu-
dents round him, whom he was entertaining with wit, and keeping from their ftudies, if not fpiriting them up to rebellion
againft the college difcipline, which, in
his maturer years, he fo much extolled."
The account of his conduct given by Dr.
Adams, who was at leaft his nominal tutor for fome time before he quitted the
college, is more favourable to his happinefs, but is lefs true. "Johnfon," fays
he, "while he was at Pembroke College,
was careffed and loved by all about him;
he was a gay and frolicfome fellow, and
paffed there the happieft part of his life."

But his own comment upon this opinion, when mentioned to him by Mr Bofwell, fhows how fallacious it is to eftimate human happinefs by external appearances: " Ah Sir, I was mad and violent. It was bitternefs which they miftook for frolic. I was miferably poor, and I thought to fight my way by my literature and my wit; fo I difregarded all power, and all authority."

He ftruggled for another year in this unequal conflict, and profeffed a defire to practife either the Civil or the Common Law; but his debts in college increafing, and his fcanty remittances from Litchfield, which had all along been made with great difficulty, being difcontinued, his father having fallen into a ftate of infolvency, he was compelled, by irrefiftible neceffity, to relinquifh his fcheme, and left the college in autumn 1735, without a degree, having been a member of it little more than three years. This was a circumstance; which, in the subsequent part of his life, he had occasion to regret, as the want of it was an obstacle to his obtaining a settlement, whence he might have derived that subsistence of which he was certain by no other means.

From the university he returned to his native city; destitute, and not knowing how he should gain even a decent livelihood. But he was so far fortunate, that the respectable character of his parents, and his own merit, secured him a kind reception in the best families of Litchfield. Mr. Gilbert Walmsley, Register of the Prerogative Court at Litchfield, " was one of the first friends that Literature procured" him; and he passed much time in the families of Mr. Howard, and Dr. Swinfen, Mr. Simpson, Mr. Levett, and Captain Garrick, father of the great ornament of the British stage. He has drawn the character of Mr. Walmsley in his " Life of Smith,"

in the glowing colours of gratitude, inter-
mingled with the dark hues of political
prejudice. In his abhorrence of whiggifm,
he has imputed to his friend and benefactor, " all the virulence and malevolence
of his party." Yet Mr. Walmfley, whofe
real character is a noble one, loved Johnfon enough to endure in *him* the principles he defpifed.

In the circles of Litchfield, he was frequently in the company of ladies, particularly at Mr. Walmfley's, whofe wife and
fifter-in-law, of the name of Afton, and
the daughters of a Baronet, were remarkable for elegance and good breeding. Of
Mifs Molly Afton, who was afterwards
married to Captain Brodie of the Navy,
he ufed to fpeak with the warmeft admiration. " Molly" (faid he) " was a
beauty and a fcholar, a wit and a whig, and
fhe talked all in praife of liberty; and fo

İ made this epigram upon her.   She was
the lovelieſt creature I ever ſaw!

> Liber ut eſſe velim, ſuaſiſti, pulchra Maria,
> Ut maneam liber; pulchra Maria, vale."

Of this epigram, Mrs. Piozzi, and Mr.
Joddrel, and Mr. Boſwell, among others,
have offered tranſlations.   The following
verſion is given by Mr. Boſwell:

> Adieu Maria! ſince you'd have me free:
> For who beholds thy charms, a ſlave muſt be.

In December 1731, his father died, in
the 79th year of his age, in very narrow
circumſtances; for, after providing for his
mother, that portion of the effects which
fell to his ſhare amounted only to twenty
pounds.

In the forlorn ſtate of his circumſtances,
he accepted the employment of uſher in
the ſchool of Market-Boſworth in Leiceſ-
terſhire, to which he went on foot, July

16. 1732. He refided in the houfe of Sir Woolfton Dixie, the patron of the fchool, to whom he officiated as a kind of domeftic chaplain; and who treated him with intolerable harfhnefs. His employment was irkfome to him in every refpect; and after fuffering for a few months, what Mr. Bofwell terms " complicated mifery," he relinquifhed a fituation which he ever afterwards remembered with a degree of horror.

Being now again totally unoccupied, he was invited by Mr. Hector to pafs fome time with him at Birmingham, as his gueft, at the houfe of Mr. Warren, with whom he lodged. Mr. Warren was the firft eftablifhed bookfeller in Birmingham, and was very attentive to Johnfon, and obtained the affiftance of his pen, in furnifhing fome periodical effays in a newfpaper of which he was proprietor.

In June 1733, he refided in the houfe of a perfon named Jarvis, in another part of the town, where he tranflated and a-bridged, from the French of the Abbé Le Grand, a *Voyage to Abyffinia*, written originally by *Jerome Lobo*, a Portuguefe Jefuit. For this work, which was printed in Birmingham, and publifhed by Bettefworth and Hitch of Pater-nofter Row, London, 8vo, 1735, but without the tranflator's, name, he had from Mr. Warren only five guineas. It is the firft profe work of Johnfon; but it exhibits no fpecimen of elegance; neither is it marked by any character of ftyle, which would lead to a difcovery of the tranflator, from an acquaintance with his latter productions. It has, however, been juftly remarked by Mr. Bofwell, that the *Preface* and *Dedication*, contain ftrong and not unfavourable fpecimens of that ftyle of thought and manner of expreffion, which he afterwards adopted.

In February 1734, he returned to Litchfield, and in Auguft following, publifhed proposals for printing by subscription an edition of the Latin poems of Politian, *Angeli Politiani Poemata Latina, quibus notas, cum historia Latinæ poeseos, a Petrarchæ ævo ad Politiani tempora deducta et vita Politiani fusius quam antehac enarrata, addidit* SAM. JOHNSON; the work to be printed in thirty 8vo sheets, price 5s. " Subscriptions taken in by the editor, or N. Johnson, bookseller of Litchfield," his brother, who had taken up his father's trade. For want of encouragement, the work never appeared, and probably never was executed.

We find him again this year at Birmingham; and in order to procure some little subsistence by his pen, he addressed a letter, under the name of *S. Smith*, to Mr. Edward Cave, the proprietor of the " Gentleman's Magazine," November 25. 1734, in which he proposed, " on reasonable terms, sometimes to supply him with

poems, inscriptions, &c. never printed before, and short literary dissertations in Latin or English, critical remarks on authors,
ancient or modern, forgotten poems that
deserve revival, loose pieces, like Floyer's,
worth preserving." To this letter Mr.
Cave returned an answer, dated December
2. 1734; but it does not appear that any
thing was done in consequence of it.

He had, from his infancy, been sensible
to the influence of female charms. When
at Stourbridge school he was much enamoured of Olivia Llyod, a young Quaker,
to whom he wrote a copy of verses;
he conceived a tender passion for Lucy
Porter, whose mother he afterwards married, and whom he had frequent opportunities of seeing at the house of Mr. Hunter of Litchfield, whose second wife was
her aunt. He addressed to her, as she herself informed Miss Seward, " when he was
a lad," the *verses to a Lady, on her presenting*

the author with a sprig of myrtle; which Mr.
Hector fays were written at his requeſt, in
1731, for his friend Mr. Morgan Graves;
but the two accounts are not irreconcileable, for he might give them to Mr. Hector, without thinking it material to mention their pre-exiſtence.

His juvenile attachments to the fair ſex
were, however, very tranſient, and he never had a criminal connection. In 1735, he
became the fervent admirer of Mrs. Porter,
widow of Mr. Henry Porter, mercer in
Birmingham, to whoſe family he had probably been introduced by his ſiſter Mrs.
Hunter of Litchfield, or through his acquaintance with Jarvis, who might be a
relation of Mrs. Porter, whoſe maiden
name was Jarvis. " It was," he ſaid, " a
love match on both ſides ;" and, judging
from the deſcription of their perſons, we
muſt ſuppoſe that the paſſion was not in-
ſpired by the beauties of form, or graces

of manner, but by a mutual admiration of each others mind. Johnſon's appearance is deſcribed as being very forbidding; " He was then lean and lank, ſo that his immenſe ſtructure of bones was hideouſly ſtriking to the eye, and the ſcars of the ſcrophula were deeply viſible. He alſo wore his hair, which was ſtraight and ſtiff, and ſeparated behind; and he often had ſeemingly convulſive ſtarts and odd geſticulations, which tended at once to excite ſurpriſe and ridicule." Mrs. Porter was double the age of Johnſon, and her perſon and manner, as deſcribed by Garrick, were by no means pleaſing to others. " She was very fat, with a boſom of more than ordinary protuberance. Her ſwelled cheeks were of a florid red, produced by thick painting, and increaſed by the liberal uſe of cordials, flaring and fantaſtic in her dreſs, and affected both in her ſpeech and in her general behaviour."

It is to be obferved, however, that whatever her real charms may have been, Johnfon thought her beautiful, for in her *Epitaph* he has recorded her as fuch; and in his *Prayers* and *Meditations*, we find very remarkable evidence that his regard and fondnefs for her never ceafed, even after death.

The marriage ceremony was performed, July 9th, at Derby, for which place the bride and bridegroom fet out on horfeback; and it muft be allowed that the capricious and fantaftic behaviour of the bride, during the journey to church, upon the nuptial morn, as related by Mr. Bofwell, was a fingular beginning of connubial felicity.

She was worth about 800l., which, to a perfon in Johnfon's circumftances, made it a defirable match. To turn this fum to the beft advantage, he hired a large houfe at Edial, near Litchfield, and fet up a private claffical academy, in which he was encouraged by his friend Mr. Walmfley. In the " Gentleman's Magazine" for 1736, there is the following " ADVERTISEMENT—At Edial, near Litchfield, in Staffordfhire, young gentlemen are boarded and taught the Latin and Greek languages, by SAMUEL JOHNSON." The plan, notwithftanding, proved abortive. The only pupils that were put under his care, were Garrick, and his brother George, and a Mr. Offely, a young gentleman of a good fortune, who died early.

About this time we find him diligently employed on his *Irene*, a tragedy, with which Mr. Walmfley was fo well pleafed, that he advifed him to proceed with it. It is founded upon a paffage in Knolles's " Hiftory of the Turks," a book which he afterwards highly praifed and recommended in the *Rambler*.

Difappointed in his expectation of deriving fubfiftence from the eftablifhment of a boarding-fchool, he now thought of trying his fortune in London, the great field of genius and exertion, where talents of every kind have the fulleft fcope, and the higheft encouragement.

On the 2d of March 1737, being the 28th year of his age, he fet out for London, and it is a memorable circumftance, that his pupil Garrick went thither at the fame time, with intention to complete his education, and follow the profeffion of the law. They were recommended to Mr. Colfon, mafter of the mathematical fchool at Rochefter, by a letter from Mr. Walmfley, who mentions the joint expedition of thefe two eminent men to the metropolis, in the following manner:

" This young gentleman, and another neighbour of mine, one Mr. Samuel Johnfon, fet out this morning for London together. Davy Garrick is to be with you early the next week, and Mr. Johnſon, to try his fate with a tragedy, and to ſee to get himſelf employed in ſome tranſlation, either from the Latin or the French. Johnſon is a very good ſcholar and poet, and I have great hopes will turn out a fine tragedy writer."

How he employed himſelf upon his firſt coming to London, is not certainly known. His firſt lodgings were at the houſe of Mr. Norris a ſtaymaker in Exeter-Street, in the Strand. Here he found it neceſſary to practiſe the moſt rigid economy; and his *Ofellus* in the *Art of Living in London*, is a real character of an Iriſh painter, who initiated him in the art of living cheaply in London.

Soon after his arrival in London, he renewed his acquaintance with Mr. Henry Hervey, one of the branches of the Briſtol family, whom he had known when he was quartered at Litchfield as an officer of the army. At his houſe he was entertained with a kindneſs and hoſpitality of which he ever afterwards retained a warm re-membrance. Not very long before his death, he deſcribed this early friend " Har-ry Hervey," thus: " he was a vicious man, but very kind to me. If you call a dog *Hervey*, I ſhall love him."

He had now written three acts of his *Irene;* and he retired for ſome time to lodgings at Greenwich, where he proceed-ed in it ſomewhat farther, and uſed to compoſe walking in the Park ; but he did not ſtay long enough in that place to finiſh it.

At this period, he wiſhed to engage more cloſely with Mr. Cave, and propoſed to him, in a letter dated Greenwich, July 12. 1737, to undertake a tranſlation of Fa-ther Paul Sarpi's " Hiſtory of the Council of Trent," from the French edition of Dr.

Le Courayer. His propofal was accepted ;
but it fhould feem from this letter, though
fubfcribed with his own name, that he had
not yet been introduced to Mr. Cave.

In the courfe of the fummer, he returned to Litchfield, where he had left his wife ;
and there he at laft finifhed his tragedy ;
which was not executed with his rapidity
of compofition upon other occafions, but
was flowly and painfully elaborated. The
original unformed fketch of this tragedy,
partly in the raw materials of profe, and
partly worked up in verfe, in his own hand-
writing, is preferved in the King's Library.

In three months after, he removed to
London with his wife ; but her daughter,
who had lived with them at Edial, was left
with her relations in the country. His
lodgings were for fome time in Wood-
ftock-Street, near Hanover-Square, and afterwards in Caftle-Street, near Cavendifh-
Square. His tragedy being, as he thought,

completely finifhed, and fit for the ftage, he folicited Mr. Fleetwood, the manager of Drury-Lane Theatre, to have it acted at his houfe; but Mr. Fleetwood would not accept it.

Upon his coming to London, he was inlifted by Mr. Cave, as a regular coadju-tor in his magazine, which, for many years, was his principal refource for employment and fupport. A confiderable period of his life is loft in faying that he was the hire-ling of Mr. Cave. The narrative is little diverfified by the enumeration of his con-tributions. But the publications of a wri-ter, like the battles and fieges of a general, are the circumftances which muft fix the feveral eras of his life. In this part of the narrative, the pieces acknowledged by Johnfon to be of his writing, are printed in Italics, and thofe which are afcribed to him upon good authority, or internal evi-

dence, are diftinguifhed by inverted com-
mas.

His firft performance in the " Gentleman's Magazine," was a Latin Ode; *Ad
Urbanum*, in March 1738, a tranflation of
which, by an unknown correfpondent, appeared in the Magazine for May following.

At this period, the misfortunes and mif-
conduct of Savage had reduced him to the
loweft ftate of wretchednefs as a writer for
bread; and his vifits at St. John's Gate,
where the " Gentleman's Magazine" was
originally printed, naturally brought Johnfon and him together. Johnfon commenced an intimacy with this extraordinary
man. Both had great parts, and they were
equally under the preffure of want. They
had a fellow-feeling, and fympathy united
them clofer.

It is melancholy to reflect, that Johnfon and Savage were fometimes in fuch

extreme indigence, that they could not pay for a lodging, fo that they have wandered together whole nights in the ftreets. Yet as Savage had feen life in all its varieties, and been much in the company of the ftatefmen and wits of his time, we may fuppofe, in thefe fcenes of diftrefs, that he communicated to Johnfon an abundant fupply of fuch materials as his philofophical curiofity moft eagerly defired, and mentioned many of the anecdotes with which he afterwards enriched the life of his unhappy companion.

He mentioned to Sir Jofhua Reynolds, that one night in particular, when Savage and he walked round St. James's Square, for want of a lodging, they were not at all depreffed by their fituation, but in high fpirits; and, brimful of patriotifm, traverfed the Square for feveral hours, inveighed againft the minifter, and " refolved they would *ftand by their country*."

Sir John Hawkins suppofes that " Johnfon was captivated by the addrefs and de-
meanour of Savage, who, as to his exterior,
was to a remarkable degree accomplifhed ;
he was a handfome well made man, and
very courteous in the modes of faluta-
tion." He took off his hat, he tells us,
with a good air, made a graceful bow, and
was a good fwordfman. " Thefe accom-
plifhments," he adds, " and the eafe and
pleafantry of his converfation, were probably the charms that wrought on Johnfon, who at this time had not been accuftomed to the converfation of gentlemen."
But if, according to his biographer's notion, he " never faw the charms of his
wife," how fhould he perceive the graces
of Savage ?

Johnfon, indeed, defcribes him as having " a graceful and manly deportment,
a folemn dignity of mien, but which, upon
a nearer acquaintance, foftened into an

engaging eaſineſs of manners." How highly he admired him for that knowledge,
which he himſelf ſo much cultivated, and
what kindneſs he entertained for him, appears in the following verſes in the Gentleman's Magazine for April 1738.

*Ad RICARDUM SAVAGE Arm. humani generis
amatorem.*

Humani ſtudium generis cui pectore fervet,
O ! colat humanum te foveatque genus !

About this time he became acquainted
with Miſs Elizabeth Carter, the learned
tranſlator of " Epictetus," to whom he paid
a friendly attention, and in the ſame Magazine complimented her in *An Ænigma
to Eliza,* both in Greek and Latin. He
writes Mr. Cave, " I think ſhe ought to be
celebrated in as many different languages
as Lewis le Grand." His verſes *to a Lady,*
(Miſs Molly Aſton) *who ſpoke in defence of
liberty,* firſt appeared in the ſame Magazine.

In May 1738, he publifhed his *London, a Poem*, written in imitation of the 3d fatire of Juvenal. It has been generally faid, that he offered it to feveral bookfellers, none of whom would purchafe it. Mr. Cave, at laft, communicated it to Dodfley, who had tafte enough to perceive its uncommon merit, and thought it " creditable to be concerned with it." Dodfley gave him 10l. for the copy. It is remarkable, that it came out on the fame morning with Pope's fatire, intituled, " 1738," One of its warmeft patrons was General Oglethorpe. Pope alfo was fo ftruck with its merit, that he fought to difcover the author, and prophefied his future fame. " He will," faid he, " foon be *deterré*," and it appears from his note to Lord Gower, he himfelf was fuccefsful in his inquiries. To " a fhort extract from *London*," in the Gentleman's Magazine for May, is added, " Become remarkable for having got to the fecond edition in the fpace of a week." This admirable poem laid the firft foundation of his fame. Sir John Hawkins obferves, that in this poem he has adopted the vulgar topic of the time, to gratify the malevolence of the Tory faction; and Mr. Bofwell candidly allows, that " the flame of patriotifm and zeal for popular refiftance with which it is fraught, had no juft caufe." It contains the moft fpirited invectives againft tyranny and oppreffion, the warmeft predilection for his own country, and the pureft love of virtue, interfperfed with traits of his own particular character and fituation. He heated his mind with the ardour of Juvenal, and he wrote with the fpirit and energy of a fine poet, and a fharp critic of the times. Boileau had imitated the fame fatire with great fuccefs, applying it to Paris; but an attentive comparifon will fatisfy every reader that he is much excelled by Johnfon. Oldham had alfo imitated it, and applied it to London; but there is fcarcely any coincidence between the two performances, though upon the very fame fubject.

In the courfe of his engagement with Mr. Cave, he compofed the *Debates in the Senate of Magna Lilliputia*, the firft number of which appeared in the " Gentleman's Magazine" for June 1738, fometimes with feigned names of the feveral fpeeches, fometimes with denominations formed of the letters of their real names, fo that they might be eafily decyphered. Parliament then kept the prefs in a kind of myfterious awe, which made it neceffary to have recourfe to fuch devices. The debates for fome time were brought home and digefted by Guthrie, and afterwards fent by Mr. Cave to Johnfon for his revifion. When Guthrie had attained to a greater variety of employment, and the fpeeches were more and more enriched by the acceffion of Johnfon's genius, it was refolved that he fhould do the whole himfelf, from notes furnifhed by perfons employed to attend in both houfes of Parliament. His fole compofition of them began November 19. 1740, and ended February 23. 1742-3. From that time they were written by Hawkefworth to the year 1760. Johnfon acknowledged the debates to be fpurious, long after the world had confidered them as genuine; and fome days previous to his death, declared, that of all his writings they gave him the moft uneafinefs. The deceit, however, could not be very per-nicious, in the effects of which fo many perfons were involved. Neither are they fo completely his own compofition as is generally fuppofed. That notes of the fpeeches were taken in the Houfes of Par-liament, and given to him, is evident from his own declarations. And it does not appear probable that Mr. Cave, who was ever attentive to the improvement of his Magazine, fhould be more negligent in procuring notes as accurate as he could, during the time when Johnfon executed this department, than when it was in the hands of Guthrie. It feems at leaft moft likely, therefore, that the language and il-luftrations are Johnfon's own, but that the arguments and general arrangements were taken from the feveral fpeeches fpoken in either Houfe.

The trade of writing was, however, fo little profitable, that notwithftanding the fuccefs of his *London*, he wifhed to accept an offer made to him, of becoming mafter of the free fchool at Appleby in Leicefter-fhire (Pope fays in Shropfhire), the falary of which was fixty pounds a-year. But the ftatutes of the fchool required that he fhould be a Mafter of Arts, and it was then thought too great a favour to be afked of the Univerſity of Oxford. Pope, without any knowledge of him, but from his *London*, recommended him to Lord Gower, who, by a letter which has been often printed, to a friend of Swift, dated Trentham, Auguſt 1. 1738, endeavoured to procure him a degree from Trinity-College, Dublin. This expedient failed. There is reaſon to think that Swift declined to meddle in the buſineſs; and to this circumſtance Johnſon's known diſlike of Swift has been often imputed.

He made one other effort to emancipate himſelf from the drudgery of authorſhip, by endeavouring to be introduced to the bar at Doctor's Commons; but here the want of a Doctor's degree in Civil Law, was alſo an unſurmountable impediment.

He was, therefore, under the neceſſity of perſevering in that courſe into which he was forced; and we find him proſecuting his deſign of tranſlating Father Paul's

"*History of the Council of Trent*," in 2 vols. 4to, which was announced in the " Weekly Mifcellany;" October 21. 1738. Twelve fheets of this tranflation were printed off; but the defign was dropped ; for it happened, that another Samuel Johnfon, Librarian of St. Martin's in the Fields, and Curate of that parifh, had engaged in the fame undertaking, under the patronage of Dr. Pearce ; the confequence of which was, an oppofition, which mutually deftroyed each others hopes of fuccefs.

In the " Gentleman's Magazine" of this year, befides the pieces already mentioned, he gave a *Life of Father Paul* in the November Magazine, and wrote the " Preface" to the volume. The " Apotheofis of Milton, a vifion," printed in the Magazine for 1738 and 1739, given to him by Sir John Hawkins, was the production of Guthrie. The tranflation of Cronfaz's " Examination of Pope's Effay on Man," and printed by Cave in November 1738, has been afcribed to him; but Mifs Carter has lately acknowledged that fhe was the tranflator.

In 1739, befide the affiftance he gave to the *Debates in the Senate of Lilliput*, his writings in the " Gentleman's Magazine," were, *The Life of Boerhaave, An Appeal to the Public in behalf of the Editor, Verfes to Eliza, a Greek Epigram to Dr. Birch*, and " Confiderations on the cafe of Dr. Trapp's Sermons," reprinted in the Magazine for July 1787.

The fame year he joined in the clamour againft Walpole, and publifhed his famous Jacobite pamphlet intituled, *Marmor Norfolcienfe, or an Effay on an Ancient Prophetical infcription in Monkifh rhyme, lately difcovered near Lynne, in Norfolk, by Probus Britannicus*. In this performance, he inveighs againft the Brunfwick fucceffion, and the meafures of Government confequent upon it,

with warm anti-Hanoverian zeal. The Jacobite principles inculcated by it, according to Sir John Hawkins, aroufed the vigi-
lance of the Miniftry. A warrant was iffued, and meffengers were employed to
apprehend the author, who, it feems, was
known. To elude his purfuers, he retired
with his wife to Lambeth-marfh, and there
lay concealed in an obfcure lodging till
the fcent grew cold. Mr. Bofwell however denies that there is any foundation
for this ftory; for that Mr. Steele, one of
the late fecretaries of the Treafury, had
directed every poffible fearch to be made
in the records of the Treafury and Secre-
tary of State's Office, but could find no
trace of any warrant having been iffued
to apprehend the author of this pamphlet.
His *Marmor Norfolcienfe* obtained alfo the
honour of Pope's commendation, as appears from the following note concerning
Johnfon, copied with minute exactnefs, by

Mr. Boſwell, from the original in the poſ-
ſeſſion of Dr. Percy.

" This [*London*] is imitated by one Johnſon, who put in for a public ſchool in
Shropſhire, but was diſappointed. He has
an infirmity of the convulſive kind, that
attacks him ſometimes, ſo as to make him
a ſad ſpectacle. Mr. P. from the merit of
this work, which was all the knowledge he
had of him, endeavoured to ſerve him
without his own application ; and wrote to
my Lord Gower, but he did not ſucceed ;
Mr. Johnſon publiſhed afterwards another
poem in Latin, with notes, the whole very
humorous, called the Norfolk Prophecy."

In the ſame year 1739, he publiſhed *A*
complete Vindication of the Licenſers of the
Stage, from the malicious and ſcandalous aſper-
ſions of Mr. Brooke, author of Guſtavus Vaſa,
in 4to. This was an ironical, but a very
proper attack upon the Lord Chamber-
lain, for the injuſtifiable ſuppreſſion of

that tragedy. Indeed the power vefted in that officer, refpecting dramatic pieces, is a difgrace to a free country; and the act which gave him that power ought to be repealed. To juftify the rejection of this play, Sir John Hawkins felects a few paf-fages, not one of which would give um-brage at this day.

In July 1739, a fubfcription was com-pleted for Savage, who was to retire to Swanfea; and he parted with the compa-nion of his midnight rambles, never to fee him more. This feparation was per-haps a real advantage to Johnfon. By affo-ciating with Savage, who was habituated to the licentioufnefs and diffipation of the town, Johnfon, though his good principles remained fteady, did not entirely preferve that temperance for which he was remark-able, in days of greater fimplicity, but was imperceptibly led into fome indulgences, which occafioned much diftrefs to his vir-

tuous mind. It is faid by Sir John Hawkins, that during his connection with Savage, a fhort feparation took place between
Johnfon and his wife. They were, however, foon brought together again. Johnfon loved her, and fhowed his affection in
various modes of gallantry, which Garrick
ufed to mimic. The affectation of fa-
fhionable airs did not fit eafy on Johnfon ;
his gallantry was received by the wife with
the flutter of a coquette, and both, we may
believe, expofed themfelves to ridicule.

In 1740, he contributed to the " Gentleman's Magazine," the " Preface," *Life
of Admiral Blake,* and the firft parts of
thofe of *Sir Francis Drake,* and of *Philip
Barettier,* both which he finifhed the year
after; An " Effay on Epitaphs," and an
Epitaph on Philips, a mufician, which was
afterwards publifhed, with fome other
pieces, in Mifs Williams's " Mifcellanies."

In 1741, he wrote for the " Gentle-man's Magazine," the " Preface," conclu-fion of his *Lives of Drake and Barettier;* " A free tranflation of the Jefts of Hiero-cles, with an Introduction," " Debate on the propofal of Parliament to Cromwell, to affume the title of King, abridged, me-thodized, and digefted; " Tranflation of Abbé Guyon's Differtation on the Ama-zons; " Tranflation of Fontenelle's Pane-gyric on Dr. Morin." He, this year, and the two following, wrote the *Parliamentary Debates.* The eloquence, the force of ar-gument, and the fplendour of language difplayed in the feveral fpeeches, are well known, and univerfally admired: To one who praifed his impartiality, obferving that he had dealt out reafon and eloquence with an equal hand to both parties, " That is not quite true, Sir, faid Johnfon; I faved appearances well enough, but I took care that the WHIG DOGS fhould not have the beft of it." They have been collected in 2 vols. 8vo, 1787, and recommended to the notice of parliamentary fpeakers, as orations upon queftions of public import- ance, by a " Preface," written by George Chalmers, Efq. whofe commercial and bio- graphical writings are well known and e- fteemed.

In 1742, he wrote for the " Gentle- man's Magazine," the " Preface;" the *Par- liamentary Debates*; *Effay on the Account of the Conduct of the Duchefs of Marlborough*, then the popular topic of converfation; *The Life of Peter Burman*; *Additions to his Life of Barettier*; *The Life of Sydenham*, af- terwards prefixed to Swan's edition of his works; the " Foreign Hiftory," for De- cember; " Effay on the Defcription of China, from the French of Du Halde; *Propofals for printing Bibliotheca Harlecana; or, a Catalogue of the Library of the Earl of Oxford*. It was afterwards prefixed to the firft volume of the " Catalogue," in which the Latin account of books were written by him. He was employed in this bufinefs by Mr. Thomas Ofborne, bookfeller in Gray's Inn; who purchafed the library for 13,000l. a fum which, Mr. Oldys fays, in one of his manufcripts, was not more than the binding of the books had coft; yet the flownefs of the fale was fuch, that there was not much gained by it. It has been confidently related, with many embellifhments, that Johnfon knocked Ofborne down in his fhop with a folio, and put his foot upon his neck. Johnfon himfelf relates it differently to Mr. Bofwell. " Sir, he was impertinent to me, and I beat him; but it was not in his fhop, it was in my own chamber." This anecdote has been often told to prove Johnfon's ferocity; but merit cannot always take the fpurns of the unworthy with patience and a forbearing fpirit.

He wrote in the " Gentleman's Magazine" for 1743, the " Preface ;" the *Parliamentary Debates* for January and February;
" Confiderations on the Difpute between
Cronfaz and Warburton, on Pope's Eflay
on Man," in which he defends Cronfaz;
Ad Lauram parituram Epigramma; *A Latin
tranflation of Pope's Verfes on his Grotto*; an
exquifitely beautiful *Ode on Friendfhip*; and
an " Advertifement" for Ofborne, concerning the Harleian Catalogue.

The fame year he wrote for his fchool-
fellow, Dr. James's " Medicinal Dictionary," in 3 vols. folio, the *Dedication to Dr.
Mead*, which is conceived with great addrefs, to conciliate the patronage of that
very eminent man. He had alfo written,
or affifted in writing, the propofals for this
work; and, being very fond of the ftudy of
phyfic, in which Dr. James was his mafter,
he furnifhed fome of the articles.

At this time, his circumſtances were much embarraſſed; yet ſuch was his liberal affection for his mother, that he took upon himſelf a debt of her's, to Mr. Levett of Litchfield, which, though only twelve pounds, was then conſiderable to him.

In 1744, he wrote the " Preface" for the Gentleman's Magazine, and the *Preface to the Harleian Miſcellany.* The ſelection of the pamphlets of which it was compoſed was made by Mr. Oldys, a man of eager curioſity, and indefatigable diligence, to whom Engliſh literature owes many obligations.

The ſame year he produced one work fully ſufficient to maintain the high reputation which he had acquired. This was the *Life of Savage*, which he had announced his intention of writing in the " Gentleman's Magazine," for Auguſt 1743. It is ſaid by Sir John Hawkins, that he compoſed the whole of it in thirty-ſix hours;

but Mr. Bofwell ftates, upon Johnfon's own authority, that he compofed forty-eight of the prefent octavo pages at a fitting, but that he fat up all night. It came out in February, from the fhop of Roberts, who, in April following, republifhed his *Life of Barettier*, in a feparate pamphlet. It was no fooner publifhed than the following liberal praife was given to it by Fielding, in " The Champion," which was copied into the " Gentleman's Magazine" for April, and confirmed by the approbation of the public.

" This pamphlet is, without flattery to its author, as juft and well-written a piece of its kind as I ever faw. It is certainly penned with equal accuracy and fpirit, of which I am fo much the better judge, as I knew many of the facts to be ftrictly true, and very fairly related. It is a very amufing, and withal a very inftructive and valuable performance. The author's obſervations are ſhort, ſignificant, and juſt, as his narrative is remarkably ſmooth, and well diſpoſed. His reflections open to all the receſſes of the human heart; and, in a word, a more juſt or pleaſant, a more engaging, or a more inſtructive treatiſe on all the excellencies and defects of human nature, is ſcarce to be found in our own, or perhaps any other language."

Johnſon had now lived nearly half his days, without friends or lucrative profeſſion; he had toiled and laboured, yet ſtill, as he himſelf expreſſes it, was " to provide for the day that was paſſing over him." Of the profeſſion of an unfriended author he ſaw the danger and the difficulties. Amhurſt, who had conducted " The Craftſman," Savage, Boyſe, and others who had laboured in literature, without emerging from diſtreſs, were recent examples, and clouded his proſpect.

Sir John Hawkins has preferved a lift of literary projects, not lefs than thirty-nine articles, which he had formed in the courfe of his ftudies; but fuch was his want of encouragement, or the verfatility of his temper, that not one of all his fchemes was ever executed.

A new edition of Shakfpeare now occurred to him, and, as a prelude to it, in April 1745, he publifhed a pamphlet, intituled *Mifcellaneous Obfervations on the Tragedy of Macbeth, with Remarks on Sir Thomas Hanmer's edition of Shakfpeare; to which is affixed, propofals for a new edition of Shakfpeare, with a Specimen,* 8vo. The notice of the public was, however, not excited to His anonymous propofals for the execution of a tafk which Warburton was known to have undertaken; the project, therefore, died at that time, to revive at a future period. His pamphlet, however, was highly efteemed, and even the fupercilious War-

burton, in the " Preface" to his Shakfpeare, publifhed two years afterwards, had
the candour to exempt it from his general
cenfure " of thofe things which have been
publifhed under the titles of " Effays," " Remarks," " Obfervations," &c. on " Shakfpeare," and fpoke of it as the work of
" a man of great parts and genius.". This
obligation Johnfon always acknowledged
in terms of gratitude. " He praifed me
(faid he) at a time when praife was of value to me."

In the year 1746, which was marked
by a civil war in Britain, when a rafh attempt was made to reftore the houfe of
Stuart to the throne, his literary career
appears to have been almoft totally fufpended. His attachment to that unfortunate family is well known ; fome may imagine that a fympathetic anxiety impeded
the exertion of his intellectual powers ;
but it is probable that he was, during that

time, employed upon his *Shakfpeare*, or fketching the outlines of his *Dictionary of the Englifh Language.*

Having formed and digefted the plan of his great philological work, which might then be efteemed one of the defiderata of Englifh literature, he communicated it to the public, in 1747, in a pamphlet intitu-led, *The Plan of a Dictionary of the Englifh Language, addreffed to the Right Honourable Philip Dormer, Earl of Chefterfield, one of his Majefty's Secretaries of State.* The hint of undertaking this work is faid to have been firft fuggefted to Johnfon by Dodfley, who contracted with him for the execution of it in conjunction with Mr. Charles Hitch, Mr. Andrew Millar, the two Meffrs. Long-man, and the two Meffrs. Knapton. The price ftipulated was 1575l.

The *Plan* has not only the fubftantial merit of comprehenfion, perfpicuity, and precifion, but the language of it is unexceptionably excellent; and never was there a more dignified ftrain of compliment than that in which he courts the atten -- tion of Chefterfield, who was very ambibitious of literary diftinction, and who, upon being informed of the defign, had expreffed himfelf in terms very favourable to its fuccefs. The way in which it came to be infcribed to Chefterfield was this: " I had neglected," fays he, " to write it by the time appointed. Dodfley fuggefted a defire to have it addreffed to Lord Chefterfield. I laid hold of this as a pretext for delay, that it might be better done, and let Dodfley have his defire." The *Plan* itfelf, however, proves that the Earl not only favoured the defign, but that there had been a particular communication with his Lordfhip concerning it.

To enable him to complete this vaft undertaking, he hired a houfe in Gough-Square, Fleet-Street, fitted up one of the

upper rooms after the manner of a count-
ing-houfe, and employed fix amanuenfes
there in tranfcribing ; five of whom were
natives of North Britain, Mr. Macbean, author of " A Syftem of Ancient Geogra-
phy," &c. Mr. Shiels, the principal col-
lector and digefter of the materials for the
" Lives of the Poets 1753," to which the
name of Mr. Theo. Cibber is prefixed ;
Mr. Stewart, fon of Mr. George Stewart,
bookfeller in Edinburgh ; and a Mr. Mait-
land : the fixth was Mr. Peyton, a French
mafter, who publifhed fome elementary
tracts. The words, partly taken from o-
ther dictionaries, and partly fupplied by
himfelf, having been firft written down,
with fpaces left between them, he delivered in writing their etymologies, definitions, and various fignifications. The authorities were copied from the books
themfelves, in which he had marked the

paffages with a black lead pencil; the traces of which could eafily be effaced.

This year he contributed to the " Gentleman's Magazine," for May, five fhort poetical pieces. " A tranflation of a Latin Epitaph on Sir Thomas Hanmer," " To Mifs ——, on her giving the author a gold and filk net-work purfe of her own weaving," " Stella in Mourning," " The Winter's Walk," " An Ode," and " To Lyce, an elderly Lady," diftinguifhed by three afterifks. In the Magazine for December, he inferted an *Ode on Winter*, which is one of the beft of his lyric compofitions.

In September, this year, his fortunate pupil, Garrick, having become joint-patentee and manager of Drury-lane theatre, he furnifhed him with a *Prologue* at the opening of it, which, for juft and manly criticifm, as well as for poetical excellence, is unrivalled in that fpecies of compofition.

In 1748, while he was employed in his *Dictionary*, he exerted his talents in occasional composition, very different from lexicography, and formed a club that met at Horseman's chop-house in Ivy-lane, Pater-noster Row, every Tuesday evening, with a view to enjoy literary discussion, and the pleasure of animated relaxation. The members associated with him in this little society, were his beloved friend, Dr. Richard Bathurst, a physician, Dr. Hawkesworth, Dr. Salter, father of the late master of the charter-house, Mr. Ryland, a merchant, Mr. John Payne, then a bookseller in Pater-noster Row; Mr. Samuel Dyer, a learned young man, intended for the dissenting ministry, Dr. William M'Ghie, a Scotch physician, Dr. Edmund Barker, a young physician, and Sir John Hawkins. The endowments of Mr. Dyer are represented by Sir John Hawkins as of such a superior kind, " that in some instances

Johnson might almoſt be ſaid to have looked up to him." They uſed to diſpute in
this club, about the *moral ſenſe* and the *fit-
neſs of things*, but Johnſon was not uniform
in his opinions; contending as often for
victory as truth. This infirmity attended
him through life.

In this year he publiſhed, in the " Gentleman's Magazine" for May, *The Life of
Roſcommon*, which has ſince been inſerted
in his " Lives of the Poets." He wrote
alſo the *Preface* to Dodſley's " Preceptor,"
and the *Viſion of Theodore, the Hermit of Te-
neriffe, found in his cell*, a moſt beautiful
allegory of human life, under the figure
of aſcending the mountain of exiſtence,
which he himſelf thought the beſt of his
writings.

In January 1749, he publiſhed *The Vanity of Human Wiſhes, being the tenth Satire
of Juvenal imitated*, with his name. Of this
poem, he compoſed ſeventy lines in one

day, without putting one of them upon paper till they were finifhed. He received of Dodfley, for the copy, only fifteen guineas. It has been thought to have lefs of common life, and more of a philofophic dignity than his *London*. It is characterized by profound reflection, more than pointed fpirit. It has, however, always been held in high efteem, and is certainly as great an effort of ethic poetry as any language can fhow. The inftances of the variety of difappointment are chofen fo judicioufly, and painted fo ftrongly, that the moment they are read, they bring conviction to every thinking mind.

On the 8th of February this year, his tragedy of *Irene*, which had been long kept back for want of encouragement, was brought upon the ftage at Drury-Lane, by the kindnefs of Garrick. A violent difpute arofe between him and the manager, relative to the alterations neceffary to be

made to fit it for the theatre. The poet
for a long time refufed to fubmit his lines
to the critical amputation of the actor, and
the latter was obliged to apply to Dr. Taylor to become a mediator in the difpute.
Johnfon's pride at length gave way to alterations; but whether to the full extent
of the manager's wifhes, is not known.
Dr. Adams was prefent the firft night of
the reprefentation, and gave Mr. Bofwell
the following account: "Before the cur-
tain drew up, there were catcalls whiftling,
which alarmed Johnfon's friends. The
prologue, which was written by himfelf,
in a manly ftrain, foothed the audience,
and the play went off tolerably till it came
to the conclufion, when Mrs. Pritchard,
the heroine of the piece, was to be
ftrangled upon the ftage, and was to fpeak
two lines with the bow ftring round her
neck. The audience cried out, " Murder! Murder!" She feveral times attempt-

ed to fpeak, but in vain. At laſt ſhe was obliged to go off the ſtage alive." This paſſage was afterwards ſtruck out, and ſhe was carried off to be put to death behind the ſcenes, as the play now has it. Mr. Boſwell aſcribes the epilogue to Sir William Yonge; but upon no good foundation.

In the unfavourable deciſion of the public upon his tragedy, Johnſon acquieſced without a murmur. He was convinced that he had not the talents neceſſary to write ſuccefsfully for the ſtage, and never made another attempt in that ſpecies of compoſition.

In December this year, he wrote the *Preface* and *Poſtſcript* to Lauder's " Eſſay on Milton's Uſe, and Imitation of the Moderns, in his Paradiſe Loſt," 8vo, a book made up of forgeries, and publiſhed to impoſe upon mankind. Sir John Hawkins tells us, that Johnſon aſſiſted Lauder from motives of enmity to the memory of Milton; but it appears, that while Lauder's work was in the prefs, the proof fheets were fubmitted to the infpection of the Ivy-Lane Club. If Johnfon approved of the defign, it was no longer than while he believed it founded in fact. With the reft of the club, he was in one common error. As foon as Dr. Douglas, now Bifhop of Salifbury, efpoufed the caufe of truth, and with ability that will ever do him honour, dragged the impoftor to open daylight, Johnfon made ample reparation to the genius of Milton. He not only difclaimed the fraud, but infifted on the impoftor confeffing his offence; and for this purpofe drew up a recantation, which Lauder figned and publifhed, intituled, " A letter to the Rev. Mr. Douglas, occafioned by his Vindication of Milton," by William Lauder, M. A. 4to, 1751. The franknefs of this confeffion would

have made some atonement for the base-
ness of the attempt, and its abject humi-
lity been deemed a sufficient punishment
of the impostor, if that unhappy man had
not had the folly and wickedness afterwards to deny this apology, and reassert
his former accusation, in a pamphlet intituled, " King Charles Vindicated from
the Charge of Plagiarism, brought against
him by Milton, and Milton himself con-
victed of Forgery and a gross imposition
on the Public," 8vo, 1755. This effort
of spleen and malice was also abortive;
and Lauder soon afterwards retired to
Barbadoes, where he died, as he had lived,
an object of general contempt, in 1771.

On the 20th March 1750, he published
the first paper of the *Rambler*, and continued it without interruption every Tuesday and Friday, till the 17th of March
1752, when it closed. In carrying on this
periodical publication, he seems neither

to have courted, nor to have met with much affiftance, the number of papers contributed by others amounting only to five in number, four billets in No. 10, by Mrs. Chapone, No. 30, by Mrs. Talbot, No. 97, by Richardfon, and Nos. 44. and 100, by Mifs Carter. Thefe admirable effays, we are told by Mr. Bofwell, were written in hafte, juft as they were wanted for the prefs, without even being read over by him before they were printed.

Making every allowance for powers far exceeding the ufual lot of man, ftill there are bounds which we muft fet to our belief upon this head. It is not at every feafon that the mind can concentrate its faculties to a particular fubject with equal ftrength, or that the fancy can create imagery fpontaneoufly to adorn and enforce its reafonings. That Johnfon fometimes felected his fubject, culled his images, and arranged his arguments for thefe papers, is evident from the notes of his common-place book, preferved by Sir John Hawkins and Mr. Bofwell. When he planned fome effays with fuch minute carefulnefs, it is not likely that he trufted wholly to the fudden effufions of his mind for the remainder. Thofe which are taken from the notes of his common-place book, do not manifeft by an excellence fuperior to the reft, peculiar labours of mind in the conception, or pains in the compofition ; and we cannot fuppofe a man fo happy in his genius, that the new-born offspring of his brain fhould invariably appear as ftrong and perfect as thofe which have been matured, fafhioned, and polifhed by fedulous reflection. This, therefore, appears to be moft probable, with refpect to the wonderful faculty which he is faid to have manifefted in this and other of his works ; that during his fleeplefs nights and frequent abftractions from company, he con-

ceived and fketched much of an impending work; that though he had in fome
degree preconceived his materials, he com-
mitted nothing to paper, juft as he is known
to have done in compofing his *Vanity of
Human Wifhes.* If this fuppofition ftrips
the account of wonder, it invefts it with
probability, fince a man of his powers of
mind and habits of compofition, might
well write an effay at a fitting, and without a blot, when he had little more to attend to, than to clothe his conceptions in
vigorous language, modulated into fonorous periods.

The *Rambler* was not fuccefsful as a periodical work, not more than five hundred
copies of any one number having been
ever printed. Of courfe, the bookfeller,
who paid Johnfon four guineas a-week,
did not carry on a very fuccefsful trade;
his generofity and perfeverance are to be
commended. While it was coming out

in single papers at London, Mr. James Elphinstone suggested, and took the charge of an edition at Edinburgh, which followed progressively the London publication, printed by Sands, Murray and Cochrane, with uncommon elegance, upon writing paper, of a duodecimo size, and was completed in eight volumes. Soon after the first folio edition was concluded, it was published in four octavo volumes; and Johnson lived to see a just tribute of approbation paid to its merit in the extensiveness of its sale, ten numerous editions of it having been printed in London, before his death, besides those of Ireland and Scotland.

This year he wrote a *Prologue*, which was spoken by Garrick, before the acting of " Comus," at Drury-Lane theatre; April 5, for the benefit of Mrs. Elizabeth Foster, Milton's grand-daughter, and the only surviving branch of his family, and

took a very zealous intereft in the fuccefs of the charity. Tonfon, the bookfeller, gave 20l. and Dr. Newton brought
a large contribution ; yet all their efforts,
joined to the allurements of Johnfon's pen,
and Garrick's performance, procured only
130l.

In 1751, while he was employed both
on the *Rambler* and his *Dictionary*, he wrote
the *Life of Cheynell*, in " The Student, or
the Oxford and Cambridge Mifcellany,"
a periodical work, in which Smart, Colman, Thornton, and other wits of both
the univerfities, diftinguifhed their talents.

Sir John Hawkins relates, that in the
fpring of this year, he indulged himfelf
in a frolic of midnight revelry. This was
to celebrate the birth of Mrs. Lennox's
firft literary child, the novel of " Harriet
Stuart." He drew the members of the
Ivy-Lane Club, and others, to the number of twenty, to the Devil Tavern, where

Mrs. Lennox and her hufband met them. Johnfon, after an invocation of the mufes, and fome other ceremonies of his own in-vention, invefted the authorefs with a laurel crown. The feftivity was protracted till morning, and Johnfon through the night was a Bachanalian, without the ufe of wine.

Though his circumftances, at this time, were far from being eafy, he received as a conftant vifitor at his houfe, Mifs Anna Williams, daughter of a Welfh phyfician, and a woman of more than ordinary talents and literature, who had juft loft her fight. She had contracted a clofe intimacy with his wife; and after her death, fhe had an apartment from him, at all times when he had a houfe. In 1755, Garrick gave her a benefit, which produced 200l. In 1766, fhe publifhed a quarto volume of " Mifcellanies," and thereby increafed her little ftock to 300l. This, and Johnſon's protection, ſupported her during the reſt of her life. :

In 1752, he republiſhed his verſion of Pope's *Meſſiab*, in the Gentleman's Magazine. Soon after his cloſing the *Rambler*, March 2, he ſuffered a loſs which affected him with the deepeſt diſtreſs. On the 17th of March, O. S. his wife died ; and after a cohabitation of ſeventeen years, left him a childleſs widower, abandoned to ſorrow, and incapable of conſolation. She was buried in the chapel of Bromley in Kent, under the care of his friend, Dr. Hawkeſworth, who reſided at that place. In the interval between her death and burial, he compoſed a *funeral ſermon* for her, which was never preached ; but, being given to Dr. Taylor, has been publiſhed ſince his death. With the ſingularity of his prayers for *Tetty*, from that time to the end of his life, the world is ſufficiently acquainted. By her firſt huſband fhe left a daughter, and a fon, a captain in the navy, who, at his death, left 10,000l. to his fifter.

On this melancholy event Johnfon felt the moft poignant diftrefs. She is, however, reported not to have been worthy of this fincere attachment. Mrs. Defmoulins, who lived for fome time with her at Hampftead, told Mr. Bofwell, that fhe indulged herfelf in country air and nice living, at an unfuitable expence, while her hufband was drudging in the fmoke of London; that fhe was negligent of economy in her domeftic affairs; and that fhe by no means treated him with that complacency which is the moft engaging quality in a wife. But all this is perfectly compatible with his fondnefs for her; efpecially when it is remembered, that he had a high opinion of her underftanding; and that the impreffion which her beauty, real, or imaginary, had originally made upon his imagination, being continued by habit, had not been effaced, though fhe herfelf was, doubtlefs, much altered for the worfe. Sir John Hawkins has declared himfelf inclined to think, " that if this fondnefs of Johnfon for his wife was not diffembled, it was a leffon that he had learned by rote; and that when he practifed it, he knew not where to ftop, until he became ridiculous." To argue from her being much older than Johnfon, or any other circumftances, that he could not really love her, is abfurd; for love is not a fubject of reafoning, but of feeling; and, therefore, there are no common principles upon which one can perfuade another concerning it. That Johnfon married her for love is believed. During her life he was fond and indulgent. At her death he was agonized; and, ever after, cherifhed her image as the companion of his moft folemn hours. If feventeen years paffed in

acts of tendernefs during their union, and
a longer period fpent in regret after death
had divided them, cannot fix our opinion
that Johnfon's fondnefs was not the effect
of diffimulation, or the unfelt leffon of a
parrot, where fhall we fix bounds to fuf-
picion, or place limits to the prefumption
of man, in paffing fentence upon the feelings of his neighbour ?

The following authentic and artlefs account of his fituation after his wife's death,
was given to Mr. Bofwell, by Francis Bar-
bar, his faithful negro-fervant, who was
brought from Jamaica by Colonel Bathurft,
father of his friend Dr. Bathurft, and
came into his family about a fortnight
after the difmal event.

" He was in great affliction :—Mifs Williams was then living in his houfe, which
was in Gough-Square. He was bufy with
his *Dictionary*; Mr. Shiels, and fome others
of the gentlemen who had formerly writ-

ten for him, used to come about him. He
had then little for himself; but frequently sent money to Mr. Shiels, when in dif-
tress. The friends who visited him at that
time, were chiefly Dr. Bathurst, and Mr.
Diamond, an apothecary in Cork-Street,
Burlington-Gardens, with whom he and
Miss Williams generally dined every Sunday. There was a talk of his going to
Ireland with him, which would probably have happened had he lived. There
were also Mr. Cave, Dr. Hakesworth, Mr.
Ryland merchant on Tower-hill, Mrs.
Masters the poetess, who lived with Mr.
Cave, Mrs. Carter, and sometimes Mrs.
Macaulay; also Mrs. Gardiner, wife of a
tallow-chandler in Snowhill, not in the
learned way, but a worthy good woman;
Mr. (now) Sir Joshua Reynolds, Mr. Millar, Mr. Dodsley, Mr. Bouquet, Mr. Payne
of Pater-noster Row, bookseller; Mr.

Strahan the printer ; the Earl of Orrery;
Lord Southwell, Mr. Garrick, &c."

Johnſon ſeems to have ſought a remedy
for this deprivation of domeſtic ſociety,
in the company of his acquaintance, the
circle of which was now very extenſive.
Among his more intimate companions at
this time, are to be reckoned, Dr. Ba-
thurſt, Dr. Hakeſworth, Sir Joſhua Reynolds; and Bennet Langton, Eſq. and
Topham Beauclerck, Eſq. eldeſt ſon of
Lord Sidney Beauclerck, young men of
elegant manners, who conceived for him
the moſt ſincere veneration and eſteem.
Innumerable were the ſcenes in which
he was amuſed by them, who, though
their opinions and modes of life were different, formed an agreeable attachment.

Mr. Boſwell has given the following account of an adventure of Johnſon's, with
his gay companions, which diſplays the
author of the *Rambler* in a new light, and

shows that his conduct was not always so solemn as his essays.

" One night when Beauclerck and Langton had supped at a tavern in London, and sat till about three in the morning, it came into their heads to go and knock up Johnson, and see if they could prevail on him to join them in a ramble. They rapped violently at the door of his chambers in the Temple, till, at last, he appeared in his shirt, with his little black wig on the top of his head, instead of a night cap, and a poker in his hand; imagining, probably, that some ruffians were coming to attack him. When he discovered who they were, and was told their errand, he smiled, and with great good humour, agreed to their proposal. " What! is it you, ye dogs! I'll have a frisk with you." He was soon dressed; and they sallied forth together into Covent-Garden, where the green grocers and fruiterers were beginning to arrange their hampers juſt come in from the country. Johnſon made ſome attempts to help them; but the honeſt gardeners ſtared ſo at his figure and man-ner, and odd interference, that he ſoon ſaw his ſervices were not reliſhed. They then repaired to one of the neighbouring taverns, and made a bowl of that liquor called *Biſhop*, which Johnſon had always liked; while in joyous contempt of ſleep, from which he had been rouſed, he re-peated the feſtive lines,

> Short, O ſhort then be thy reign,
> And give us to the world again!

" They did not ſtay long, but walked down to the Thames, took a boat, and rowed to Billingſgate. Beauclerck and John-ſon were ſo well pleaſed with their amuſe-ment, that they reſolved to perſevere in diſſipation for the reſt of the day; but Langton deſerted them, being engaged to breakfaſt with ſome young ladies."

In the catalogue of Johnfon's vifitants, given by his fervant, many are no doubt omitted ; in particular, his humble friend Robert Levett, an obfcure practifer in phy-fic amongft the lower people, with whom he had been acquainted from the year 1746. Such was his predilection for him, and fanciful eftimation of his moderate a-bilities, that he confulted him in all that related to his health, and " made him fo neceffary to him, as hardly to be able to live without him." He now drew him into a clofer intimacy with him, and not long after, gave him an apartment in his houfe ; of which he continued a conftant inmate during the remainder of his life. He waited upon him every morning through the whole courfe of his tedious breakfaft, and was feen generally no more by him till midnight. He was of a ftrange gro-tefque appearance ; ftiff and formal in his manner, and feldom faid a word while any company was prefent. He married, when he was near fixty, a ftreet-walker, who perfuaded him that fhe was a woman of family and fortune. His character was rendered valuable by repeated proofs of honefty, tendernefs, and gratitude to his benefactor, as well as by an unceafing diligence in his profeffion. His fingle failing was an occafional departure from fobriety.

In a fhort time after the *Rambler* ceafed, Dr. Hawkefworth projected the " Adventurer," in connection with Bonnel Thornton, Dr. Bathurft and others. The firft number was publifhed, November 7. 1752, and the paper continued twice a-week, till March 9. 1754. Thornton's affiftance was foon withdrawn, and he fet up a new paper, in conjunction with Colman, called the " Connoiffeur."

Johnfon was zealous for the fuccefs of the " Adventurer," which was at firft ra-

ther more fuccefsful than the *Rambler*. He
engaged the affiftance of. Dr. Warton, whofe
admirable effays are well known. April
10. 1753, he began to write in it, marking
his papers with the fignature *T;* all of
which, except thofe which have alfo the fignature *Mifargyrus* (by Dr. Bathurft), are
his. His price was two guineas for each
paper. Of all thefe papers, he gave both
the fame and the profit to Dr. Bathurft.
Indeed, the latter wrote them while Johnfon dictated ; though he confidered it as a
point of honour not to own them. He
even ufed to fay he did not *write* them, on
the pretext that he *dictated* them only ; al-
lowing himfelf, by this cafuiftry, to be " ac-
ceffary to the propagation of falfehood,"
though his confcience had been hurt by
even the appearance of impofition in writing the *Parliamentary Debates.* This year
he wrote for Mrs. Lennox, the *Dedication to*

the Earl of Orrery, of her " Shakfpeare Illuftrated," 2 vols. 12mo.

The death of Mr. Cave, January 10. 1754,
gave him an opportnity of fhewing his regard for his early patron, by writing his
Life, which was publifhed in the " Gentleman's Magazine" for February. This
feems to have been the only new performance of that year, except his papers
in the " Adventurer." In the end of July,
he found leifure to make an excurfion to
Oxford, for the purpofe of confulting the
libraries there. " He ftayed," fays Mr.
Warton, " about five weeks; but he collected nothing in the libraries for his *Dictionary*."

As the *Dictionary* drew towards a conclufion, Chefterfield, who had previoufly
treated Johnfon with unpardonable neglect
(which was the real caufe of the breach
between them, and not the commonly received ftory of Johnfon's being denied ad-

mittance while Cibber was with his lordſhip), now as meanly courted a reconcilia-
tion with him, in hopes of being immor-
talized in a dedication.   With this view,
he wrote two eſſays in " The World" in
praiſe of the *Dictionary,* and, according to
Sir John Hawkins, ſent Sir Thomas Ro-
binſon to him, for the ſame purpoſe.   But
Johnſon, who had not renounced the connection, but upon the juſt grounds of continued neglect, was ſenſible, that to liſten
to an accommodation, would be to exchange dignity for a friendſhip trifling in
its value, and precarious in its tenure. He
therefore rejected his advances, and ſpurn-
ed his proffered patronage, by the following letter, dated February 1755, which is
preſerved here as a model of courtly ſar-
caſm, and manly reprehenſion, couched in
terms equally reſpectful in their form, and
cutting in their eſſence.   It affords the
nobleſt leſſon to both authors and patrons

that ſtands upon record in the annals of literary hiſtory.

" I have been lately informed by the proprietor of " The World," that two papers in which my *Dictionary* is recommended to the public, were written by your Lordſhip. To be ſo diſtinguiſhed, is an honour, which, being very little accuſtomed to favours from the great, I know not well how to receive, or in what terms to acknowledge.

" When, upon ſome ſlight encouragement, I firſt viſited your Lordſhip, I was overpowered, like the reſt of mankind, by your addreſs, and could not forbear to wiſh that I might boaſt myſelf *Le vainqueur du vainqueur de la terre*, that I might obtain that regard for which I ſaw the world contending ; but I found my attendance ſo little encouraged, that neither pride nor modeſty would ſuffer me to continue it. When I had once addreſſed your Lordſhip in public, I had exhaufted all the art of pleafing, which a retired and uncourtly fcholar can poffefs. I had done all that I could; and no man is well pleafed to have his all neglected, be it ever fo little.

" Seven years, my Lord, have now paffed fince I waited in your outward rooms, or was repulfed from your door; during which time, I have been pufhing on my work through difficulties, of which it is ufelefs to complain, and have brought it, at laft, to the verge of publication, without one act of affiftance, one word of encouragement, or one fmile of favour. Such treatment I did not expect, for I never had a patron before.

" The Shepherd in Virgil grew at laft acquainted with Love, and found him a native of the rocks.

" Is not a patron, my Lord, one who looks with unconcern on a man ftruggling for life in the water, and, when he has reached ground, encumbers him with help? The notice which you have been pleafed to take of my labours, had it been early, had been kind : but it has been delayed till I am indifferent, and cannot enjoy it ; till I am folitary, and cannot impart it ; till I am known, and do not want it. I hope it is no very cynical afperity, not to confefs obligations where no benefit has been received, or to be unwilling that the public fhould confider me as owing that to a patron, which Providence has enabled me to do for myfelf.

" Having carried on my work thus far, with fo little obligation to any favourer of learning, I fhall not be difappointed though I fhould conclude it, if lefs be poffible, with lefs ; for I have been long wakened from that dream of hope, in which I once boafted myfelf with fo much exultation,—My Lord, your, &c."

Johnſon, however, acknowledged to Mr. Langton, that " he did once receive ten pounds from Lord Cheſterfield; but that, as that was ſo inconſiderable a ſum, he thought the mention of it could not properly find place in a letter of the kind that this was." Cheſterfield read the letter to Dodſley with an air of indifference, " ſmiled at the ſeveral paſſages, and obſerved how well they were expreſſed." He excuſed his neglect of Johnſon, by ſaying, " that he had heard he had changed his lodgings, and did not know where he lived;" and declared, " that he would have turned off the beſt ſervant he ever had, if he had known that he denied him to a man who would have been always more than welcome." Of Cheſterfield's general affability and eaſineſs of acceſs, eſpecially to literary men, the evidence is unqueſtionable; but, from the character which he gave of Johnſon, in his " Letters to his

Son" [Let. 112.], and the difference in their manners, little union or friendship could be looked for between them. Certain it is, however, that Johnson remained under an obligation to Chesterfield, to the value of *ten pounds*.

On the 10th of February, previous to the publication of his *Dictionary*, the University of Oxford, in anticipation of the excellence of this work, at the solicitation of his friend Mr. Warton, unanimously conferred upon him the degree of Master of Arts; which, it has been observed, could not be obtained for him at an early period, but was now considered as an honour of considerable importance, in order to grace the title page of his *Dictionary*.

At length, in May following, his *Dictionary*, with a *Grammar* and *History of the English Language*, was published in 2 vols. folio; and was received by the learned world, who had long wished for its appearance, with an applaufe proportionable to the impatience which the promife of it had excited. Though we may believe him, in the declaration at the end of his *Preface*, that he " difmiffed it with frigid tranquillity, having little to fear or hope from cenfure or from praife;" we cannot but fuppofe that he was pleafed " in the gloom of folitude," with the honour it procured him, both abroad and at home. The Earl of Corke and Orrery, being at Florence, prefented it to the *Academia della Crufca*. That academy fent Johnfon their *Vocabulario*, and the French Academy fent him their *Dictionaire*, by Mr. Langton. As though he had forefeen fome of the circumftances which would attend this publication, he obferves, " A few wild blunders and rifible abfurdities, from which no work of fuch multiplicity was ever free, may for a time furnifh Folly with laughter, and harden Ignorance into contempt;

but ufeful Diligence will at laft prevail, and there can never be wanting fome who diftinguifh defert." Among thofe who a-mufed themfelves and the public on this occafion, Mr. Wilkes, in an Effay printed in the Public Advertifer, ridiculed the following paffage in the *Grammar*. " H feldom, perhaps never, begins any but the firft fyllable." The pofition is undoubtedly expreffed with too much latitude; but Johnfon never altered the paffage. Dr. Kenrick's threatened attack, feveral years after, in his Review of Johnfon's *Shakfpeare*, never faw the light. Campbell's ridicule of his ftyle under the title of " Lexiphanes," 1767, and Callender's " Deformities of Dr. Johnfon," 1782, though laughable, from the application of Johnfon's " words of large meaning" to infignificant matters, are fcarcely worthy of notice. His old pupil, Garrick, complimented him on its coming out firſt, in the following " Epigram," alluding to the ill-ſucceſs of the *forty* members of the French Academy employed in ſettling their language.

> Talk of war with a Briton, he'll boldly advance
> That one Engliſh ſoldier will beat ten of France:
> Would we alter the boaſt, from the ſword to the pen,
> Our odds are ſtill greater, ſtill greater our men;
> In the deep mines of ſcience, though Frenchmen may toil,
> Can their ſtrength be compar'd to Locke, Newton, and Boyle:
> Let them rally their heroes, ſend forth all their powers,
> Their verſe-men, and proſe-men; then match them with ours;
> Fïrſt Shakſpeare and Milton, like gods in the fight,
> Have put their whole drama and epic to flight;
> In ſatires, epiſtles, and odes would they cope,
> Their numbers retreat before Dryden and Pope;
> And Johnſon, well arm'd like a hero of yore,
> Has beat *forty* French, and will beat forty more!

In this year, he afforded his aſſiſtance to Mr. Zechariah Williams, father of the blind lady whom he had humanely received under his roof, who had quitted his profeſſion in hopes of obtaining the great parliamentary reward for the diſcovering of the longitude; and benevolently wrote for him, " An account of an attempt to aſcertain the longitude at ſea, by an exact theory of the variation of the magnetical needle; with a table of the variations at the moſt remarkable cities in Europe, from the year 1660, to 1860, 4to, by Zachariah Williams." This pamphlet was publiſhed in Engliſh and Italian, the tranſlation being the work, as is ſuppoſed, of Mr. Baretti. Mr. Williams failed of ſucceſs, and died July 12. 1755, in his 83d year. Johnſon placed this pamphlet in the Bodleian library, and for fear of any omiſſion or miſtake, he entered, in the great catalogue, the title page of it, with his own hand. It appears from his correſpondence with Mr. Warton, that he " intended, in the winter 1755, to open a Biblio-

I

Neque, or Literary Journal, to be intituled, *The Annals of Literature, Foreign as well as Domeſtic*, for which he had made ſome proviſion of materials; but the ſcheme was dropped.

.Having ſpent, during the progreſs of the work, the money for which he had contracted to write his *Dictionary*, he was ſtill under the neceſſity of exerting his talents, " in making proviſion for the day that was paſſing over him." The ſubſcriptions taken in for his edition of *Shakſpeare*, and the profits of his miſcellaneous eſſays, were now his principal reſource for ſubſiſtence; and it appears from the following letter to Richardſon, dated Gough-Square, March 16. 1756, that they were inſufficient to ward off the diſtreſs of an arreſt, on a particular emergency.

" I am obliged to entreat your aſſiſtance; I am now under an arreſt for five pounds eighteen ſhillings. Mr. Strahan, from whom I fhould have received the neceffary help,. in this cafe, is not at home, and I am afraid of not finding Mr. Millar. If you could be fo good as to fend me this fum, I will very gratefully repay you, and add it to all former obligations." In the margin of this letter, there is a memorandum in thefe words:—" March 16. 1756. Sent fix guineas. Witnefs William Richardfon."

" For the honour of an admired writer," fays Mr. Murphy, " it is to be regretted that we do not find a more liberal entry." This anecdote may appear to fupport the parfimony of the author, whofe hero gives moft profufely; but fomething may ftill be. faid in favour of Richardfon. All that Johnfon afked was a temporary fupply; and that was granted. There was certainly no oftentatious liberality; but a kind action feems to have been done, without delay, and without grudging.

In 1756, he publiſhed an abridgment of his *Dictionary*, in 2 vols, 8vo, and contributed to a publication called " The Univerſal Viſitor," for the aſſiſtance of Smart, one of the ſtated undertakers, with whoſe unhappy vacillation of mind he ſincerely ſympathized, all the eſſays marked with two *aſteriſks*; except the " Life of Chaucer," " Reflections on the ſtate of Portugal," and " Eſſay on Architecture," which want all the characteriſtical marks of his compoſition. " Further thoughts on Agriculture," being the ſequel of a very inferior eſſay on the ſame ſubject," " A Diſſertation on the State of Literature and Authors," and " A Diſſertation on the Epitaphs written by Pope," though not marked in the ſame manner, appear to be the production of Johnſon. The laſt of theſe, indeed, he afterwards added to his *Idler*.

He engaged alſo to ſuperintend and contribute largely to another monthly publi-

cation, intituled, " The Literary Magazine, or Univerfal Review ;" the firft number of which came out on the 15th of
May this year.   He continued to write in
it, with intermiffions, till the 15th number.   His original effays are, " The Pre-
liminary Addrefs," " An Introduction to
the Political State of Great Britain,"
" Remarks on the Militia Bill," " Obfervations on his Britannic Majefty's Trea-
ties with the Emprefs of Ruffia, and the
Landgrave of Heffe Caffel," " Obfervations
on the Prefent State of Affairs," and " Memoirs of Frederick II. King of Pruffia."
His reviews of the works of others are,
" Birch's Hiftory of the Royal Society,"
" Murphy's Gray's-Inn Journal," " Warton's Effay on the Genius and Writings
of Pope, vol. 1ft." " Hampton's Tranflation of Polybius," " Blackwell's Memoirs
of the Court of Auguftus," " Ruffel's Natural Hiftory of Aleppo," " Sir Ifaac New-

-ton's Arguments in proof of a Deity,"
" Borlafe's Hiftory of the Ifles of Scilly,"
" Home's Experiments on Bleaching,"
" Brown's Chriftian Morals," " Hales on
Diftilling Sea-Water, &c." " Lucas's Effay on Waters," " Keith's Catalogue of
the Scottifh Bifhops," " Browne's Hiftory
of Jamaica," " Philofophical Tranfactions,
vol. 49th," " *Mrs. Lenox's Tranflation of
Sully's Memoirs*," " Mifcellanies by Elizabeth Harrifon," " Evans's Map, and Account of the Middle Colonies in America,"
" *Letter on the Cafe of Admiral Byng*,"
" *Appeal to the People concerning Admiral
Byng*," " *Hanway's Eight Day's Journey,
and Effay on Tea*," " The Cadet, a Military Treatife," " *Some further Particulars
in relation to the Cafe of Admiral Byng, by a
Gentleman of Oxford*," " The Conduct of
the Miniftry relating to the prefent War,
impartially examined," and " *Jenyns's Free
Inquiry into the Nature and Origin of Evil.*"

Mr. Davies, in his " Mifcellaneous and Fugitive Pieces," has afcribed to him the " Review of Burke's Inquiry into the Origin of our Ideas of the Sublime," and Sir John Hawkins has inferted it in his collection of Johnfon's works; but it was written by Mr. Murphy. In his original effays, he difplays extenfive political knowledge, expreffed with uncommon energy and perfpicuity. Some of his reviews are very fhort accounts of the pieces noticed; but many of them are examples of elaborate criticifm, in the moft mafterly ftyle, particularly the review of Jenyns's " Inquiry into the Origin of Evil." In his defence of Tea, againft Mr. Hanway's violent attack upon that popular beverage, he defcribes himfelf as " a hardened and fhamelefs tea-drinker, who has for many years diluted his meals with only the infufion of this facinating plant; whofe kettle has fcarcely time to cool; who with tea amuſes the evening, with tea ſolaces the midnight, and with tea welcomes the morning," *te veniente die, te decedente.* Mr. Hanway wrote an angry anſwer to Johnſon's review of his " Eſſay;" and Johnſon, after a full and deliberate pauſe, made a reply to it ; the only inſtance in the whole courſe of his life, when he condeſcended to oppoſe any thing that was written againſt him. Of the good Mr. Hanway he ſaid, " He is a man whoſe failings may be well pardoned for his virtues."

The ſame year he gave an edition of Sir Thomas Browne's " Chriſtian Morals," with his *Life* prefixed to it, which is one of his beſt biographical performances. He wrote alſo a *Dedication* and *Preface to the Earl of Rochford,* to Payne's " Eſſay on the Game of Draughts," and accepted of a guinea from Dodſley, for writing the *Introduction* to " The London Chronicle :"

and even in fo flight a performance exhibited peculiar talents. At the fame time
he iffued *Propofals* of confiderable length
for his edition of *Shakfpeare*, with Notes ;
and his fancied activity was fuch, that he
promifed his work fhould be publifhed
before Chriftmas 1757, though it was nine
years before it faw the light.

About this period, he was offered by Mr.
Langton, the father of his much valued
friend, a living of confiderable value in
Lincolnfhire, if he would accept it and
take orders ; " but he chofe not to put off
his lay habit." This year the Ivy-Lane
club was diffolved, by the difperfion of
the members.

In 1757, it does not appear that he
publifhed any thing, except fome of thofe
effays in the " Literary Magazine," which
have been mentioned. That magazine,
after he ceafed to write in it, gradually
declined ; and in July 1758, it expired.

He dictated, this year, a " Speech on the Subject of an Address to the Throne," after the expedition to Rochefort, which was delivered by one of his friends in a public meeting. It is printed in the " Gentleman's Magazine" for October 1785.

On the 15th of April 1758, he began *The Idler*, which came out every Saturday, in a weekly newspaper called the " Universal Chronicle," published by Newbery, and was continued till April 5th 1760. Of 103, the total number of essays, twelve were contributed by his friends ; of which Nos. 33, 93. and 96, were written by Mr. Warton, No. 67 by Mr. Langton, and Nos. 76, 79, and 82, by Sir Joshua Reynolds; the concluding words of No. 82, " and pollute his canvass with deformity," being added by Johnson. *The Idler* is evidently the work of the same mind which produced the *Rambler*, but has less body and more spirit. It has more variety of

real life, and greater facility of language,
Yet Nos. 14, 24, 41, 43, 51, 52, 58, and
89, fhow as much profundity of thought,
and labour of language, as any of his writings. To *The Idler*, when collected in
volumes, he added (befide the *Effay on E-
pitaphs*, and the *Differtation* on thofe of
Pope), an *Effay on the Bravery of the Englifh common Soldiers.*

In January 1759, his mother died, at
the age of ninety; an event which deeply affected him. He regretted his not having gone to vifit her for feveral years
previous to her death; but he had long
contributed liberally to her fupport.

Soon after this event, he wrote his *Raffelas, Prince of Abyffinia*, that, with the profits, he might defray the expence of his
mother's funeral, and pay fome little debts
which fhe had left. He told Sir Jofhua
Reynolds, that he compofed it in the even-
ings of one week, fent it to the prefs in

5

portions as it was written, and had never fince read it over. He received for the copy 100l. and 25l. when it came to a fecond edition. The applaufe given to the hiftory of *Ruffelas*, has been fuch, as muft fatisfy an author the moft avaricious of fame. It has been tranflated into various modern languages, and received the admiration of Europe.

During all this year, he carried on his *Idler*, and was proceeding, though flowly, in his edition of *Shakfpeare*. He, however, found time to tranflate for Mrs. Lenox's Englifh verfion of Brumoy's " Greek Theatre," " A Differtation on the Greek Comedy," and the general " conclufion" of the book. On the controverfy arifing concerning the eliptical or circular form of arches for Blackfriar's bridge, Johnfon engaged in it, on behalf of his friend Mr. Gwyn, and wrote *three letters* in the " Gazetteer," in oppofition to the eliptical fide of the queſtion ; but without any illiberal antipathy to. Mr. Mylne, with whom he afterwards lived upon very agreeable terms, of acquaintance.

While he was employed in writing *The Idler,* he quitted his houſe in Gough-Square, and retired to Gray's-Inn ; and ſoon after Miſs Williams went to lodgings. This year he removed to chambers in the Inner-Temple Lane, " where he lived," ſays Mr. Murphy, " in poverty, total idle-neſs, and the pride of literature, *Magni ſtat nominis umbra.* Mr. Fitzherbet (the father of Lord St. Helens), uſed to ſay, that he paid a morning viſit to Johnſon, intending from his chambers to ſend a letter into the city ; but, to his great ſur-priſe, he found an author by profeſſion, without pen, ink, or paper."

His black ſervant Francis Barber having left him, and entered on board a man of war, " he was humble enough to deſire the affiftance" of Smollet in procuring his releafe. Smollet made intereft through Mr. Wilkes; and he was difcharged without any wifh of his own, in the latter end of 1759, and returned to his mafter's fervice.

In 1760, he wrote the " Addrefs of the Painters to George III. on his acceffion ;" an " Introduction" to the proceedings of the Committee for Clothing the French Prifoners; the " Dedication" for Mr. Baretti, of his " Italian and Englifh Dictionary," to the Marquis of Abreu, the Spanifh ambaffador ; and an *Account of Mr. Tytler's Vindication of Mary Queen of Scots,* in the Gentleman's Magazine for October.

This year Mr. Murphy having thought himfelf ill treated by Dr. Franklin, in his " Differtation on Tragedy," publifhed an indignant vindication in " A Poetical Epiftle to Samuel Johnfon, A. M." in which he complimented Johnfon in a juft and elegant manner. This epiftle has been reprinted, with confiderable alterations and additions, in the collection of his works, in 7 vols, 8vo, 1786. As an ingenious, an elegant, and moral writer, Mr. Murphy is entitled to rank in a fuperior clafs. In collecting his works, it is to be regretted that he fhould have taken fo much pains to refcue from oblivion this epiftle, written during the violence of literary diffention, and which bears · evident marks of an exafperated mind. The expulfion of the refpectable names of Dr. Warton and Mr. Mafon from their former places, cannot eafily be defended upon any other ground than caprice, or perfonal diflike.

An acquaintance firft commenced between Johnfon and Mr. Murphy in the following manner: During the publication of his " Gray's-Inn Journal," Mr. Murphy happened to be in the country with Foote, and having mentioned that he was obliged to go to London to get ready for the prefs one of the numbers, Foote faid to him, " You need not go on that account: Here is a French magazine, in which you will find a very pretty oriental tale; tranflate that, and fend it to your printer." Mr. Murphy having read the tale, was highly pleafed with it, and followed Foote's advice. When he returned to town, this tale was pointed out to him in the *Rambler*, from whence it had been tranflated into the French Magazine. Mr. Murphy then waited upon Johnfon, to explain this curious incident; and a friendfhip was formed, that continued without interruption till the death of Johnfon.

In 1761, he wrote for the bookfellers the " Preface" to Rolt's Dictionary of Trade and Commerce; which difplays a clear and comprehenfive knowledge of the fubject, though he " never (as he faid) faw the man, and never read the book." He alfo corrected a pamphlet written by Mr. Gwyn, intituled, " Thoughts on the Coronation of George III.," and wrote for Mr. Newbery the *Introduction* to a Collection of Voyages and Travels publifhed by him, under the title of " The World Difplayed," which contains, in a pleafing ftyle, the hiftory of navigation, and the difcovery of America and the Iflands of the Weft Indies.

In 1762, he wrote for Dr. Kennedy, in a ftrain of very courtly elegance, *A Dedication to the King*, of his " Complete Syftem of Aftronomical Chronology," " Dedication" for Mrs. Lenox, to the Earl of Middlefex, of her " Female Quixotte," and the " Preface" to the " Catalogue of the Artift's Exhibition."

In this year, Fortune, who had hitherto left him to ftruggle with the inconveniences of a precarious fubfiftence, arifing entirely from his own labours, gave him that independence which his talents and virtues long before ought to have obtained for him. In the month of July he was graced with a penfion of 300 l. *per annum*, by the King, as a recompence for the honour which the excellence of his writings, and the benefit which their moral tendency had been of to thefe kingdoms. He obtained it by the interference of Lord Bute, then firft Lord Commiffioner of the Treafury, upon the fuggeftion of Mr. Wedderburn, now Lord Loughborough, at the inftance of Mr. Sheridan and Mr. Murphy. For this independence he paid the ufual tax. Envy and refentment foon made him the mark to fhoot their arrows at. Some appeared to think themfelves more entitled to royal favour, and others recollected his political opinions, and fentiments of the reigning family. By fome he was cenfured as an apoftate, and by others ridiculed for becoming a penfioner. The " North Briton" fupplied himfelf with arguments againft the Minifter for rewarding a Tory and a Jacobite, and Churchill faterized his political verfatility with the moft poignant feverity.

> How to all principles untrue,
> Not fix'd to old friends, nor to new ;
> He damns the penfion which he takes,
> And loves the Stuart he forfakes.

By this acceptance of the King's bounty, he had undoubtedly fubjected himfelf to the appellation of a penfioner, to which he had annexed an ignominious definition in his *Dictionary*. He had received a favour from two Scotchmen, againft whofe country he had joined in the rabble cry of indifcriminating invective. It was thus that even-handed Juftice commended the poisoned chalice to his own lips, and compelled him to an awkward, though not unpleasant penance, for indulging in a splenetic prejudice, equally unworthy of his understanding and his heart.

The affair itself was equally honourable to the giver and the receiver. The offer was clogged with no stipulations for party services, and accepted under no implied idea of being recompensed by political writings. It was perfectly understood by all parties, that the pension was merely honorary. It is true that Johnson did afterwards write political pamphlets in favour of administration; but it was at a period long subsequent to the grant of his pension, and in support of a minister to whom he owed no personal obligation. It was for the establishment of opinions, which, however unconstitutional, he had uniformly held, and publicly avowed.

In 1763, he furnished to "The Poetical Calendar," publifhed by Fawkes and Woty, a *Character of Collins*, which he afterwards engrafted into his entire *Life of Collins*. He alfo favoured Mr. Hoole with the *Dedication* of his tranflation of Taffo to the Queen.

This year Mr. Bofwell was introduced to Johnfon, by Mr. Davies the bookfeller, and continued to live in the greateft intimacy with him from that time till his death.

Churchill, in his "Ghoft," availed himfelf of the common opinion of Johnfon's credulity, and drew a caricature of him, under the name of *Pompofo*; reprefenting him as one of the believers of the ftory of a ghoft in Cock-Lane, which, in 1762, had gained very general credit in London. Johnfon made no reply; " for with other wife folks he fat up with the ghoft." Pofterity muft be allowed to fmile at the credulity of that period. Contrary, however, to the common opinion of Johnſon's credulity, Mr. Boſwell aſſerts that he was a principal agent in detecting the impoſture; and undeceived the world, by publiſhing an account of it in the " Gentleman's Magazine" for January 1762. Yet, by the circumſtances of the examination, he ſeems to have gone with almoſt a willingneſs to believe, and a mind ſcarcely in ſuſpenſe. He would have been glad to ſee a traveller from that undiſcovered country, over which, like the reſt of mankind, he ſaw nothing but clouds and darkneſs.

In one of the *converſations* at the Mitre Tavern this year, Mr. Boſwell relates the following inſtance of Johnſon's profound and liberal way of thinking, on a very nice conſtitutional point, which may, in ſome meaſure, render people cautious of pronouncing deciſively on his political creed,

" Goldfmith difputed very warmly with Johnfon, againft the well known maxim of the Britifh conftitution, " The king can do no wrong," affirming, that what was morally falfe, could not be politically true; and as the king might, in the exercife of his regal power, command, and caufe the doing of what was wrong, it certainly might be faid, in fenfe and in reafon, that he *could* do wrong." *Johnfon.* " Sir, you are to confider, that in our conftitution, according to its true principles, the king is the head, he is fupreme, he is above every thing, and there is no power by which he can be tried. Therefore it is, Sir, that we hold the king can do no wrong; that whatever may happen to be wrong in government may not be above our reach, by being afcribed to majefty. Redrefs is always to be had againft oppreffion, by punifh-ing the immediate agents. The king, though he fhould command, cannot force a judge to condemn a man unjuftly; therefore it is the judge whom we profecute and punifh. Political inftitutions are formed on the confideration of what will moft frequently tend to the good of the whole, although now and then exceptions may occur. Thus, it is better that a nation fhould have a fupreme legiflative power, although it may at times be abufed. And then, Sir, there is this confideration, that, *if the abufe be enormous, nature will rife up, and claiming her original right, overturn a corrupt political fyftem.*

" This generous fentiment," Mr. Bofwell adds, " which he uttered with great fervour, ftruck me exceedingly, and ftirred my blood to that pitch of fancied refiftance, the poffibility of which I am glad to keep in mind, but to which, I truft, I fhall never be forced."

In this year, he alfo wrote the " Life of Afcham," and the " Dedication to the Earl of Shaftſbury," prefixed to the edition of his Engliſh works, publiſhed by Mr. Bennet.

To enlarge his circle, and to find opportunities for converſation, Johnſon once more had recourſe to a club. In February 1764, was founded that club, which afterwards became diſtinguiſhed by the title of the LITERARY CLUB. Sir Joſhua Reynolds was the firſt propoſer, to which Johnſon acceded; and the original members were, beſide himſelf, Sir Joſhua Reynolds, Mr. Burke, Dr. Nugent, Mr. Beauclerk, Mr. Langton, Mr. Chamier, Sir John Hawkins, and Goldſmith. They met at the Turk's Head, in Gerard Street, Soho, on every Monday evening through the year.

He wrote this year " A Review" of Grainger's " Sugar Cane," in the " London Chronicle," in conjunction with Dr. Percy; and an account of Goldſmith's " Traveller," in the " Critical Review."

About this time, he was afflicted with a
fevere return of the hypochondriac diforder, which was ever lurking about him.
He was fo ill as to be entirely averfe to
fociety, the moft fatal fymptom of that
malady.

The fucceeding year, 1765, was remarkable for the commencement of his acquaintance with Henry Thrale, Efq. one
of the moft eminent brewers in England,
and member of parliament for Southwark.
Mr. Murphy, who was intimate with Mr.
Thrale, having fpoken very highly of Johnfon's converfation, he was requefted to make
them acquainted. This being mentioned
to Johnfon, he accepted an invitation to
dinner at Mr. Thrale's, and was fo much
pleafed with his reception, both by Mr.
and Mrs. Thrale, and they fo much pleafed with him, that his invitations to their
houfe were more and more frequent; till
at laft, in 1776, he became one of the fa-

mily; and an apartment was appropriated to him, both in their houfe in Southwark, and in their villa at Streatham.

Nothing could be more fortunate for Johnfon than this connection. He had at Mr. Thrale's all the comforts, and even the luxuries of life; his melancholy was diverted, and his irregular habits leffened, by affociation with an agreeable and well-ordered family. He was treated with the utmoft refpect, and even affection. Johnfon had a very fincere efteem for Mr. Thrale, as a man of excellent principles, a good fcholar, well-fkilled in trade, of a found underftanding, and of manners fuch as prefented the character of a plain independent Englifh 'fquire. He underftood and valued Johnfon, without remiffion, from their firft acquaintance to the day of his death. Of Mrs. Thrale, now Mrs. Piozzi, a lady of lively parts, improved by education, " lefs cannot be faid," fays Mr. Tyers, " than

that in one of the latter opinions of Johnfon:" " If fhe was not the wifeft woman
in the world, fhe was undoubtedly one of
the wittieft." She took fuch care of him,
during an illnefs of fome continuance, that
Goldfmith told her, " he owed his life to
her attention." " To a natural vivacity in
converfation, fhe had reading enough, and
the gods had made her poetical." The vivacity of Mrs. Thrale's literary talk rouzed
him to cheerfulnefs and attention, even
when they were alone. But this was not
often the cafe ; for he found here a conftant
fucceffion of what gave him the higheft en-
joyment. The fociety of the learned, the
witty, and the eminent in every way, who
were affembled in numerous companies,
called forth his wonderful powers, and gratified him with admiration, to which no
man could be infenfible.

There is fomething in the conduct of this
worthy poffeffor of wealth, which the mind

loves to contemplate. Next to the posses-
sion of great powers, the most enviable qualities, are a capacity to discover, and an inclination to honour them. To the credit
of Thrale, let it be recorded, that the patron of literature and talents, of which
Johnson sought in vain for the traces in
Chesterfield, he found realized in Thrale.

In July of this year, he was complimented by the University of Dublin with the
degree of Doctor of Laws, as the *Diploma*
expresses it, *ob egregiam scriptorem elegantiam
et utilitatem*, though he does not appear to
have taken the title in consequence of it.
In October, he at length gave to the world
his edition of *The Plays of William Shakspeare,
with the Corrections and Illustrations of various Commentators ; to which are added, Notes
by Sam. Johnson*, 8vo ; which, as far as it
fell short of affording that ample satisfac-
tion which was expected from it, may be
ascribed to his not having " read the books

which the author read, traced his knowledge to the fource, and compared his copies with their originals;" a promife he gave, but was not able to perform. Sir John Hawkins thinks it a meagre work; he complains of the paucity of the notes, of Johnfon's want of induftry, and indeed unfitnefs for the office of a Scholiaft. It was treated with great illiberality by Dr. Kenrick, in the firft part of a " Review" of it, which was never completed. It is to be admitted, that he has neither fo fully reformed the text, by accurate collations of the firft editions, nor fo fairly illuftrated his author, in his notes, by quotations from the " writers who lived at the fame time, immediately preceded, or immediately followed him," as has been done by other able and ingenious critics, who have followed him; Mr. Steevens, Mr. Capel, Mr. Malone, Mr. Reed, &c. whofe labours have left little to add to the commentaries on

Shakfpeare. But what he did as a commentator, has no fmall fhare of merit, though his refearches were not fo ample, and his inveftigations fo acute as they might have been. He has enriched his edition with a concife account of each play, and of its characteriftic excellence. In the fagacity of his emendatory criticifms, and the happinefs of his interpretations of obfcure paffages, he furpaffes every editor of this poet. Mr. Malone confeffes, " that Johnfon's vigorous and comprehenfive underftanding threw more light on his author, than all his predeceffors had done." His *Preface* has been pronounced by Mr. Malone, to be the fineft compofition in our language; and having regard to its fubject and extent, it certainly would be difficult to name one poffeffing a fuperior claim to fuch fuperlative praife. Whether we confider the beauty and vigour of its compofition, the abundance and claffical felec-

tion of its allufions, the juftnefs of the general precepts of criticifm, and its accurate
eftimate of the excellencies or defects of his
author, it is equally admirable. He feems
to raife his talents upon a level with thofe
of his poet, upon whofe works he fits as a
critical judge, to rival, by the luftre of his
praifes, the fplendour of the original, and to
follow this eagle of Britifh poetry through
all his gyres, with as keen an eye, and upon
as ftrong a wing. The *Preface* to his *Dictionary*, correct as it is, muft yield the palm of
excellence to that prefixed to his Shakfpeare; but it yields it only becaufe the
fubject was lefs favourable to the full difplay
of his powers.

In 1766, he removed from the Inner-
Temple Lane, to a good houfe in Johnfon's
Court, Fleet Street, in which he accommo-
dated Mifs Williams with an apartment on
the ground floor, while Mr. Levett occupied
his poft in the garret.

This year he only wrote the *Dedication to the King*, of Gwyn's " London and Weft-minfter Improved," and furnifhed the *Preface*, and the following pieces for Mifs Wil-liams's " Mifcellanies in Profe and Verfe," 4to : *The Ant*; " To Mifs ——, on her giv-ing the Author a Gold and Silk Net-work Purfe of her own weaving ;" " The Happy Life;" *On the Death of Stephen Gray, the Electrician*; and " The Fountains," a Fairy Tale, in Profe. The firft fketch of the poem on *Stephen Gray*, was written by Mifs Williams, but Johnfon told Mr. Bof-well, " that he wrote it all over again, ex-cept two lines." · This publication was en-couraged by a genteel fubfcription.

In 1767, he only wrote the *Dedication to the King*, for Mr. Adams's " Treatife on the Globes." In February, he was honoured by a private converfation with the king, in the library at Buckingham Houfe, " which gratified his monarchic enthufiafm." The interview was fought by the king without the knowledge of Johnfon. His majefty, among other things, afked the author of fo many valuable works, if he intended to publifh any more? Johnfon modeftly anfwered, that he thought he had written enough. "And fo fhould I too," replied the king, "if you had not written fo well." Johnfon was highly pleafed with his majefty's courteoufnefs; and afterwards obferved to Mr. Langton, " Sir, his manners are thofe of as fine a gentleman as we may fuppofe Lewis XIV. or Charles II."

Johnfon had now arrived at that eminence which is the prize that cultivated genius always ftruggles for, and but feldom obtains. His fortune, though not great, was adequate to his wants, and of moft honourable acquifition; for it was derived from the produce of his labours, and the rewards which his country had beftowed upon merit. He received during life that unqualified applaufe from the world, which is in general paid only to departed excellence, and he beheld his fame feated firmly in the public mind, without the danger of its being fhaken by obloquy, or the hazard of its being fhared by a rival. He could number among his friends the greateft and moft improved talents of the country. His company was courted by wealth, dignity, and beauty. His many peculiarities were overlooked, or forgotten in the admiration of his underftanding; while his virtues were regarded with veneration, and his opinions adopted with fubmiffion. Of the ufual infenfibility of mankind to living merit, Johnfon, at leaft, had no reafon to complain.

In 1768, nothing of his writing was given to the public, except the *Prologue* to his friend Goldfmith's comedy of the " Good Natured Man."

In 1769, he was altogether quiefcent as an author. On the eftablifhment of the Royal Academy this year, he accepted the title of Profeffor of Ancient Literature.

In 1770, he publifhed a political pamphlet, intituled *The Falfe Alarm*, 8vo.; intended to juftify the conduct of miniftry, and their majority in the Houfe of Commons, for having virtually affumed it as an axiom, that the expulfion of a member of parliament was equivalent to exclufion, and their having declared Colonel Luttrel to be duly elected for the county of Middlefex, notwithftanding Mr. Wilkes had a great majority of votes. This being very juftly confidered as a grofs violation of the right of election, an alarm for the conftitution extended itfelf all over the kingdom. To prove this alarm to be falfe, was the purpofe of Johnfon's pamphlet; but his arguments and eloquence failed of effect, and the Houfe of Commons has fince erafed the offenſive reſolution from the journals. This pamphlet has great merit in point of language; but it contains much groſs miſrepreſentation, and much malignity, and abounds with ſuch arbitrary principles, as are totally inconſiſtent with a free conſtitution.

The next year, 1771, he defended the meaſures adopted by the miniſtry, in the diſpute with the court of Spain, in a pamphlet, intituled *Thoughts on the late Tranſactions reſpecting Falkland's Iſland*, 8vo. On the ſubject of Falkland's Iſlands, ſpots " thrown aſide from human uſe, barren in ſummer, and ſtormy in winter," he appears to have followed the direction, and adopted the opinions which a puſillanimous adminiſtration wiſhed to inculcate. They were certainly erroneous in a political view; and if they were his own, ſhow, that on ſuch ſubjects he was incapable of forming a juſt opinion. His deſcription of the miferies of war, in this pamphlet, is a fine piece of eloquence; and his character of *Junius* is executed with all the force of his genius, and with the higheft care.

When Johnfon fhone in the plenitude of his political glory, from the celebrity of his minifterial pamphlets, an attempt was made to bring him into the Houfe of Com- mons, by Mr. Strahan, the king's printer, who was himfelf in parliament, and wrote to the fecretary of the treafury upon the fubject; but the application was unfucceff- ful. Whether there were any particular reafons for the refufal, has not tranfpired. That Johnfon very much wifhed to " try his hand" in the fenate, he has himfelf de- clared; but that he would have fucceed- ed as a parliamentary fpeaker, is at leaft doubtful. Few have diftinguifhed them- felves as orators, who have not begun the practice of fpeaking in public early in life; and it may be doubted whether the habits of regular and correct compofition are not unfavourable to that quick unpremeditated elocution, which is fo much admired, and fo ufeful in animated debate. This at leaft is certain, that of the many perfons eminent for literary abilities, who have had feats in parliament, none have gained a reputation for eloquence commenfurate with their talents and information ; and of Johnfon, in particular, it is reported upon the authority of Sir William Scott, that he had feveral times tried to fpeak in the Society of Arts, &c. but " had found that he could not get on." It was obferved by the late Henry Flood, Efq. who was himfelf an eminent orator, that " Johnfon having been long ufed to fententious brevity, and the fhort flights of converfation, might have failed in that continued and expanded kind of argument, which is requifite in ftating complicated matters in public fpeaking."

In 1772, he produced no literary performance. His only publication in 1773,
was a new edition of his *Dictionary*, with
additions and corrections. In the autumn
of 1773, he gratified a " wifh which he had
fo long entertained, that he fcarcely remembered how it was formed, of vifiting
the Hebrides, or Weftern Iflands of Scotland." He was accompanied by Mr. Bofwell, " whofe acutenefs," he afterwards obferved, " would help his inquiry, and whofe
gaiety of converfation, and civility of manners, were fufficient to counteract the in-
conveniencies of travel in countries lefs hof-
pitable than thofe they were to pafs."

His ftay in Scotland was from the 18th
of Auguft, till the 22d of November, when
he fet out on his return to London. His
various adventures, and the force and vivacity of his mind, as exercifed during his
tour, have been defcribed by Mr. Bofwell,
in his " Journal of a Tour to the Hebrides,"

8vo, 1786, in a ſtyle that ſhows he poſſeſſed, in an eminent degree, the ſkill to give connection to miſcellaneous matter, and vivacity to the whole of his narrative.

At the approach of the general election, in 1774, he publiſhed a ſhort political pamphlet, intituled, *The Patriot; addreſſed to the Electors of Great Britain*, 8vo, not with any viſible application to Mr. Wilkes, but to teach the people to reject the leaders of oppoſition, who called themſelves patriots. It was called for, he tells us, by his political friends, on Friday, and was written on Saturday.

The firſt effort of his pen, in 1775, was " Propoſals for publiſhing by ſubſcription, the works of Mrs. Charlotte Lennox, in 3 vols. 4to." which was ſoon ſucceeded by a pamphlet, intituled, *Taxation no Tyranny, An Anſwer to the Reſolutions and Addreſs of the American Congreſs*, 8vo. The ſcope of the argument was, that diſtant colonies

which had in their aſſemblies a legiſlature
of their own, were, notwithſtanding, liable
to be taxed in a Britiſh Parliament, where
they had neither peers in one houſe, nor re-
preſentatives in the other. The principle
has been long abandoned; but Johnſon
was of opinion, that this country was ſtrong
enough to enforce obedience; " When,"
ſays he " an Engliſhman is told that the
Americans ſhoot up like a hydra, he naturally conſiders how the hydra was deſtroy-
ed." The event has ſhown how much he
was miſtaken. This pamphlet was written at the deſire of the miniſtry, and in
ſome places corrected by them. It con-
tained the ſame poſitive aſſertions, ſarcaſti-
cal ſeverity, extravagant ridicule, and arbitrary principles, with his former political
pieces, and the groſſeſt and moſt virulent
abuſe of the Americans.

Theſe pamphlets were publiſhed on his
own account, and were afterwards collect-

ed by him into a volume, under the title of *Political Tracts, by the author of the Rambler,* 8vo, 1775.

In the month of March this year, he was gratified by the title of Doctor of Laws, conferred on him by the Univerſity of Oxford, at the ſolicitation of Lord North. In September he viſited France, for the firſt time, with Mr. and Mrs. Thrale, and Mr. Baretti; and returned to England in about two months after he quitted it. Foote, who happened to be in Paris at the ſame time, ſaid, that the French were perfectly aſtoniſhed at his figure and manner, and at his dreſs; which was exactly the ſame with what he was accuſtomed to in London: his brown clothes, black ſtockings, and plain ſhirt. Of the occurrences of this tour, he kept a journal, in all probability with a deſign of writing an account of it. The world has to regret, that from want of leifure or inclination, he never perfected it.

This year he alfo wrote the Preface to Mr. Baretti's " Leffons, Italian and Eng-lifh," and publifhed an account of his Tour to the Hebrides, under the title of *A Jour-ney to the Weftern Iflands of Scotland*, 8vo. This elegant narrative has been varioufly praifed and abufed in the newfpapers, ma-gazines, and other fugitive publications. It was formally attacked by the Rev. Do-nald M'Nicol, in his " Remarks," &c. 8vo. 1780. That it is written with an undue prejudice againft both the country and people of Scotland, muft be allowed; but it abounds in extenfive philofophical views of fociety, and in ingenious fentiments and lively defcription. Among many other difquifitions equally inftructing and amuf-ing, he expreffes his difbelief of the au-thenticity of the poems of Offian, prefent-ed to the public as a tranflation from the

Erſe, in ſuch terms as honeſt indignation
is apt to hurl againſt impoſition.   If there
was a manuſcript, in what age was it written? and where is it?   If it was collected
from oral recitation in different parts of
the Highlands, who put it together in its
preſent form?   Theſe, and ſuch like obſervations, provoked the reſentment of Mr.
Macpherſon; he ſent a threatening letter
to the author, and Johnſon anſwered him
in the rough phraſe of ſtern defiance.

" I received your fooliſh and impudent
letter.   Any violence offered me, I ſhall
do my beſt to repel; and what I cannot
do for myſelf, the law ſhall do for me.   I
hope I ſhall never be deterred from detecting what I think a cheat, by the menaces
of a ruffian.

" What would you have me retract?   I
thought your book an impoſture; I think
it an impoſture ſtill.   For this opinion I
have given my reaſons to the public, which

I here dare you to refute. Your rage I defy. Your abilities, fince your Homer, are not fo formidable; and what I hear of your morals, inclines me to pay regard not to what you fhall fay, but what you fhall prove. You may print this if you will."

The threats alluded to in this letter never were attempted to be put in execution. But Johnfon, as a provifion for defence, furnifhed himfelf with a large oaken plant, fix feet in height, of the diameter of an inch at the lower end, increafing to three inches at the top, and terminating in a head (once the root) of the fize of a large orange. This he kept in his bed-chamber, fo near his chair, as to be within his reach.

In 1776, he wrote nothing for the public. This year he removed from No. 7. Johnfon's Court, to a larger houfe, No. 8. Bolt-Court, Fleet-Street, with a garden, " which he took delight in watering." A room on the ground-floor was affigned to Mifs Williams; and the whole of the two pair of ftairs floors was made a repofitory for his books, confifting of about 5000 volumes. Here, in the intervals of his refidence at Streatham, he fat every morning receiving vifits, and hearing the topics of the day, and indolently trifling away the time; and to the moft intimate of his friends, Dr. Burney, Mr. Hoole, Mr. Murphy, Mr. Davies, Mr. Baretti, Mr. Bofwell, Mr. Langton, &c. fometimes gave not inelegant dinners. Chemiftry afforded fome amufement. In Gough-Square, and in Johnfon's-Court, he had an apparatus for that purpofe; and the fame, with perhaps a few additions, was now fixed up in Bolt-Court. He had alfo a fort of laboratory at Streatham, and diverted himfelf with drawing effences, and colouring liquors for Mrs. Thrale.

Johnson's benevolence to the unfortunate, was, at all periods of his life, very remarkable. In his house at Bolt-Court, an apartment was appropriated to Mrs. Defmoulins, daughter of his god-father, Dr. Swinfen, and widow of Mr. Defmoulins, a writing-mafter, and her daughter, and a Mifs Carmichael. Such was his humanity, and fuch his generofity, that he allowed Mrs. Defmoulins half-a-guinea a-week, which was above a twelfth part of his penfion.

" It feems," fays Mrs. Piozzi, " at once vexatious and comical, to reflect that the diffenfions thofe people chofe to live in, diftreffed and mortified him exceedingly. He really was oftentimes afraid of going home, becaufe he was fure to be met at the door with numberlefs complaints; and he ufed frequently to lament pathetically to me, and to Mr. Saftres, the Italian mafter, who was much his favourite, that they made his life miferable, from the impoffibility he found of making theirs happy ; when every favour he beftowed on one, was wormwood to the reft. If, however, I ventured to blame their ingratitude, and condemn their conduct, he would inftantly fei about foftening the one, and juftifying the other ; and finifhed commonly by telling me, that I knew not to make allowances for fituations I never experienced:

> To thee no reafon, who know'ft only good,
> But evil haft not try'd.   *Milton.*"

In 1777, the fate of Dr. Dodd excited Johnfon's compaffion, and called forth the ftrenuous exertion of his vaft comprehenfive mind. He thought his fentence juft ; yet, perhaps, fearing that religion might fuffer from the errors of one of its minifters, he endeavoured to prevent the laft ignominious fpectacle. He wrote for that unhappy man, his *Speech to the Recorder of*

London, at the Old Bailey, when the sentence of death was about to be pronounced upon him; *The Convict's Address to his unhappy Brethren*, a sermon delivered by him in the chapel of Newgate; two *Letters*, one to Lord Chancellor Bathurst, and one to Lord Mansfield; *A Petition from Dr. Dodd to the King; A Petition from Mrs. Dodd to the Queen; Observations* in the newspapers on occasion of Earl Percy's having presented a petition for mercy to Dodd, signed by twenty thousand people; *A Petition from the City of London;* and Dr. Dodd's *Last Solemn Declaration*, which he left with the sheriff at the place of execution.

In the summer, he wrote a *Prologue* to Kelly's comedy of " A Word to the Wife," acted at Covent-Garden Theatre, for one night, for the benefit of the author's widow and children. He also made some *additions* to the life of Bishop Pearce (who assisted him with some etymologies in the compilation of his Dictionary), prefixed to his posthumous works, in 2 vols. 4to, and wrote the *Dedication to the King*.

This year he engaged to write a concise account of the *Lives of the English Poets*, whose works were inserted in an edition undertaken by the London bookfellers, at that time, in oppofition to the edition of the " Britifh Poets," printing by the Martins at Edinburgh, and to be fold by Mr. Bell in London. As a recompence for an undertaking, as he thought, " not very tedious or difficult," he bargained for two hundred guineas ; and was afterwards prefented by the proprietors with one hundred pounds. His defign was only to have allotted to every poet an *Advertifement*, like that which we find in the French mifcellanies, containing a few dates, and a general character, which would have conferred not much reputation upon the writer, nor have communicated much information to

his readers. Happily for both, " the ho-
neft defire of giving ufeful pleafure," led
him beyond his firft intention. In execut-
ing this limited defign, he found his attention fo much engaged, that he enlarged his
fcheme, and entered more fully into the
merits and value of the principal writers;
and produced an ample, rich, and entertaining view of them in every refpect. The
firft four volumes of this work were publifhed in 1779, under the title of *Biographical and Critical Prefaces*, and the remaining five in 1781. " Some time in March,"
he fays, in his *Meditations*, " I finifhed the
Lives of the Poets, which I wrote in my
ufual way, dilatorily and haftily; unwilling
to work, and working with vigour and
hafte." In a memorandum previous to
this, he fays of them : " Written, I hope,
in fuch a manner, as may tend to the pro-
motion of piety."

In the selection of the poets he had no responsible concern; but Blackmore, Watts, Pomfret, and Yalden, were inserted by his recommendation; and Mr. Nichols tells us, he was frequently confulted during the printing of the collection, and revifed many of the fheets.

This was the laft of Johnfon's literary labours; and though completed when he was in his feventy-firft year, fhows that his faculties were in as vigorous a ftate as ever. His judgment and his tafte, his quicknefs in the difcrimination of motives, and facility of moral reflection, fhine as ftrongly in thefe narratives, as in any of his more early performances; and his ftyle, if not fo energetic, is at leaft more fmoothed down to the tafte of the generality of critical objectors.

The *Lives of the Englifh Poets* formed a memorable era in Johnfon's life. It is a work which has contributed to immor-

-talize his name, and has fecured that rational efteem which party or partiality could not procure, and which even the injudicious zeal of his friends has not been able to leffen.

From the clofe of his laft great work, the malady that perfecuted him through life, came upon him with redoubled force. His conftitution declined faft, and the fabric of his mind feemed to be tottering. The contemplation of his approaching end was conftantly before his eyes; and the profpect of death, he declared, was terrible.

On the 4th of May 1781, he loft his valuable friend Thrale, who appointed him one of his executors, with a legacy of 200l. " I felt," he faid, " almoft the laft flutter of his pulfe, and looked for the laft time upon the face that, for fifteen years, had never been turned upon me but with refpect and benignity." Of his departed friend he has given a true character in a Latin *Epitaph*, to be feen in the church of Streatham.

With Thrale, many of the comforts of Johnfon's life may be faid to have expired. In the courfe of 1782, he complains that he " paffed the fummer at Streatham, but there was no Thrale." In the fame year, he received another fhock. He was fuddenly deprived of his old domeftic companion Levett, and paid a tribute to his memory in an affecting and characteriftic *Elegy*.

The fucceffive loffes of thofe acquaintances whom kindnefs had rendered dear, or habit made neceffary to him, reminded Johnfon of his own mortality.

After the death of Thrale, his vifits to Streatham, where he no longer looked upon himfelf as a welcome gueft, became lefs and lefs frequent; and on the 5th of April 1783, he took his final leave of Mrs. Thrale, to whom, for near twenty years, he was under the higheſt obligations.

" The original reaſon of our connection," ſays Mrs. Piozzi, in her lively and entertaining " Anecdotes," his *particularly diſordered health and ſpirits*, had been long at an end. Veneration for his virtues, reverence for his talents, delight in his converſation, and habitual endurance of a yoke my huſband firſt put upon me, and of which he contentedly bore his ſhare for ſixteen or ſeventeen years, made me go on ſo long with Mr. Johnſon ; but the perpetual confinement, I will own to have been terrifying in the firſt years of our friendſhip, and irkſome in the laſt ; nor would I pretend to ſupport it without help, when my coadjutor was no more."

A friendly correſpondence continued, however, between Johnſon and Mrs. Thrale, without interruption, till the ſummer following, when ſhe retired to Bath, and informed him, that she was going to dispose of herself in marriage to Signior Piozzi, an Italian music master. Johnson, in his relation of executor to her husband, as also in gratitude to his memory, was under an obligation to promote the welfare of his family. He endeavoured, therefore, by prudent counsels and friendly admonition, to prevent that which he thought one of the greatest evils which could befal the children of his friend, the alienation of the affections of their mother. " The answer to his friendly monition," says Sir John Hawkins, " I have seen; it is written from Bath, and contains an indignant vindication, as well of her conduct as her fame, an inhibition of Johnson from following her to Bath, and a farewel, concluding, " Till you have changed your opinion of ————, let us converse no more." In his last letter, 8th July 1784, directed to Mrs. *Piozzi,* who then had announced her marriage to him, he fays, " I breathe out one figh more of tendernefs, perhaps ufelefs, but at leaft fincere." He gives her his beft advice, and adds, " the tears ftand in my eyes."

Excluded from the dwelling and family of his friend, he was compelled to return to his own houfe, to fpend cheerlefs hours among the objects of his bounty, when increafing age and infirmities had made their company more obnoxious than when he left them, and the fociety of which he had been recently deprived, rendered him, by comparifon, lefs patient to endure it.

From this time, the narrative of his life is little more than a recital of the preffures of melancholy and difeafe, and of numberlefs excurfions, taken to calm his anxiety, and foothe his apprehenfions of the terrors of death, by flying, as it were, from himfelf. He was now doomed to feel all thofe calamities incident to length of days, which he had fo eloquently enumerated in his *Vanity of Human Wifhes.*

On the 17th of June 1783, he was afflicted with a paralytic ftroke, which deprived him of fpeech; from which, however, he gradually recovered; fo that in July he was able to make a vifit to Mr. Langton, at Rochefter; and made little excurfions, as eafily as at any time of his life.

In September, while he was on a vifit at Heale, the feat of Mr. Bowles, in Wiltfhire, he loft Mrs. Williams, whofe death he lamented with all the tendernefs which a long connection naturally infpires. This was another fhock to a mind like his, ever agitated with the dread of his own diffolution.

Befides the palfy, he was all this year afflicted with the gout, as well as with a *farcocele*, which he bore with uncommon firmnefs.

In December, he fought a weak refuge from anxiety, in the inftitution of a weekly club, at the Effex Head, in Effex Street, then kept by an old fervant of Mr. Thrale's; but the amufement which he promifed himfelf from this inftitution, was but of fhort duration.

In the beginning of the year 1784, he was feized with a fpafmodic afthma, which was foon accompanied by fome degree of dropfy. From the latter of thefe complaints, however, he was greatly relieved by a courfe of medicine.

The interval of convalefcence, which he enjoyed during the fummer, induced him to exprefs a wifh to vifit Italy. Upon this fubject, however, his wifhes had been anticipated by the anxiety of his friends to preferve his health. His penfion not being deemed by them adequate to fupport the expence of the journey, application was made to the minifter, by Mr. Bofwell and Sir Jofhua Reynolds, unknown to Johnfon, through Lord Chancellor Thurlow, for an augmentation of it, by 200l. The application was unfuccefsful; but the Chancellor, in the handfomeft manner, offered to let him have 500l. from his own purfe, under the appellation of a loan, but with the intention of conferring it as a prefent. It is alfo to be recorded to the honour of Dr. Brocklefby, that he offered to contribute 100l. per annum, during his refidence abroad. Johnfon, however, declined both thefe offers, with a gratitude and dignity of fentiment, rifing almoft to an equal elevation with the generofity of Lord Thurlow, and Dr. Brocklefby; and, indeed, he was now approaching faft to a ftate in which money could be of no avail.

In the beginning of July, he fet out on a vifit to Dr. Taylor, at Afhbourn in Derbyfhire, where his complaints appear to have met with but little alleviation. From Derbyfhire he proceeded to Litchfield, to take a laft view of his native city. After leaving Litchfield, he vifited Birmingham and

Oxford, and arrived in London on the 16th of November.

The fine and firm feelings of friendfhip which occupied fo large a portion of John-fon's heart, were eminently difplayed, in the many tender interviews which took place between him and his friends in the country, during his excurfion into the North: an excurfion which feems to have been undertaken rather from a fenfe of his approaching diffolution, and a warm wifh to bid thofe he loved a laft and long fare-wel, than from any rational hope that air and exercife would reftore him to his for-mer health and vigour.

Soon after his return to London, both the afthma and dropfy became more violent and diftrefsful. Eternity prefented to his imagination an awful profpect, and with as much virtue as in general is the lot of man, he fhuddered at the approach of his diffolu-tion. He felt ftrong perturbations of mind.

His friends endeavoured all in their power
to awaken the comfortable reflections of a
life well spent. They prayed with him; and
Johnson poured out occafionally the warmeft effufions of piety and devotion.

He had for fome time kept a journal in
Latin of the ftate of his illnefs, and the remedies which he ufed, under the title of
Ægri Ephemeris, which he began on the 6th
July, but continued it no longer than the
8th November, finding, perhaps, that it was
a mournful and unavailing regifter.

His attention to the caufe of literature
was evinced, among other circumftances,
by his communicating to Mr. Nichols a lift
of the original authors of " The Univerfal
Hiftory," mentioning their feveral fhares
in that work. It has, according to his direction, been depofited in the " Britifh Mu-
feum," and is printed in the Gentleman's
Magazine for December 1784. His integrity was evinced, by paying a fmall debt

to Mr. Faden, which he had borrowed of his father, and a larger one to Mr. Hamilton.. But the queſtion will recur, why were theſe debts ſo long ſuffered to remain ? for we cannot ſuppoſe that his mind was ſuddenly enlightened, and his memory renovated.

During his ſleeplefs nights, alſo, he amuſed himſelf by tranſlating into Latin verſe, from the Greek, many of the *Epigrams* in the *Anthologia*.

The ſenſe of his ſituation predominated, and " his affection for his departed relations," ſays Mr. Boſwell, " ſeemed to grow warmer, as he approached nearer to the time when he might hope to ſee them again." In a letter to Mr. Green, at Litchfield, 2d December 1784, he encloſed the *Epitaph* on his father, mother, and brother, and ordered it to be engraved on a ſtone, " deep, maffy, and hard," and laid on " the exact place of interment," in the middle aifle of St. Michael's church. In the Summer he laid a ftone with a Latin *Epitaph* over his wife in the chapel of Bromley, in Kent.

During his illnefs, he experienced the fteady and kind attachment of his numerous friends. Nobody was more attentive to him than Mr. Langton, to whom he tenderly faid, *Te teneam moriens, deficiente manu.* Dr. Heberden, Dr. Brocklefby, Dr. Warren, Dr. Butter, and Mr. Cruikfhank, generoufly attended him without accepting any fees; and all that could be done from profeffional fkill and ability, was done, to prolong a life fo truly valuable. But his conftitution was decayed beyond the reftorative powers of the medical art. Unfortunately for him, he himfelf had a fmattering of the medical fcience; and imagining that the dropfical collection of water which oppreffed him, might be drawn off, by making incifions in the calves of his legs, with his ufual defiance of pain, cut deep, when he thought Mr. Cruikfhank had done it too tenderly. An effufion of blood followed, which brought on a dozing. Previous to his diffolution, he burnt indifcriminately large maffes of paper, and among others, two quarto volumes, " containing a full and moft particular Account of his own Life," the lofs of which is much to be regretted. The laft days of this great man's exiftence appear to have been unclouded by the gloomy apprehenfions which he had formerly entertained. Full of refignation, ftrengthened in faith, and joyful in hope, on the 13th of December, in the evening, being in the 75th year of his age, he refigned his breath with fo much compofure, that his death was only known by the ceafing of his refpiration, which had been rendered difficult by debility and afthma. He was buried in Weftminfter-Abbey, near the foot of Shakfpeare's monument, and clofe to the coffin of his friend Garrick: His funeral was attended by a refpectable number of his friends; particularly by many of the members of the LITERARY CLUB, who were then in town, and feveral of the reverend Chapter of Weftminfter. His fchool-fellow and friend, Dr. Taylor, read the funeral fervice. Agreeable to his own requeft, a large blue flag-ftone was placed over his grave, with this infcription :

SAMUEL JOHNSON, LL. D.
Obiit XIII die Decembris
Anno Domini
M DCC LXXXV.
Ætatis fuæ LXXV.

A monument for Johnfon, in the Cathedral church of St. Paul's, in conjunction with the illuftrious Howard, was refolved upon, with the approbation of the Dean and Chapter, in 1789, and has been fup-

ported by a moſt reſpectable contribution.
It is in ſuch forwardneſs, that it is expected to be opened in October 1795.

Having no near relations, he left the
bulk of his property, amounting to 1500l.
to his faithful ſervant, Francis Barber,
whom he looked upon as particularly under his protection, and whom he had all a-
long treated as an humble friend. He appointed Sir Joſhua Reynolds, Sir John Hawkins, and Dr. (now Sir) William Scott, his
executors.

His death attracted the public attention
in an uncommon degree, and was followed
by an unprecedented accumulation of literary honours, in the various forms of Sermons, Elegies, Memoirs, Lives, Eſſays, and
Anecdotes. A ſermon on that event was
preached before the Univerſity of Oxford,
by Mr. Augutter; and Dr. Fordyce, in his
" Addreſſes to the Deity," 12mo, 1785,
and an " Epitaph" printed in the " Gen-

tleman's Magazine" for 1785, paid an elegant and affectionate tribute to his memory. The " Elegy on the Death of Dr. Johnson," by Samuel Hobhouse, Esq. 4to, 1785, was distinguished from the mass of elegiac verses on that occasion; and the just, discriminative, and elegant " Poetical Review of the Moral and Literary Character of Dr. Johnson," by John Courtenay, Esq. M. P. 4to, 1788, was perused with avidity by the admirers of wit and learning, and the real friends of virtue and liberty. His conduct and genius were examined and illustrated in the rapid " Biographical Sketch of Dr. Johnson," by Thomas Tyers, Esq. in the " Gentleman's Magazine" for 1784; the sprightly and entertaining " Anecdotes of Dr. Johnson," by Mrs. Piozzi, 8vo, 1785; the candid and judicious " Essay on the Life, Character, and Writings of Dr. Johnson," by Joseph Towers, LL. D. 8vo, 1786; and the instructive and inte-

.refting " Life of Samuel Johnfon, LL. D."
by James Bofwell, Efq. 2 vols. 4to, 1791,
which are fufficiently known to the world.

His *Works* were collected and publifhed by
Sir John Hawkins, with his " Life," in
eleven volumes, 1787. In this edition, the
Lives of the Poets are placed firft, and feveral pieces are attributed to Johnfon without foundation. In the " Life," too much
foreign matter is intermixed, and Johnfon
himfelf is fcarcely vifible in the mafs. A
new edition was publifhed in 12 vols. 8vo,
1792, with an " Effay on his Life and Genius," by Arthur Murphy, Efq., the former
" Life" being thought too unwieldy for re-
publication. In this edition, the order obferved in the former edition is inverted, and
the feveral pieces are chronologically arranged, omitting thofe attributed to him
without foundation. Some of his *Prayers*
are printed, and feveral of his *Letters* added to the 12th volume. Mr. Murphy has

no new facts to embellish his work ; but the task which has been left him, of giving a short, yet full, a faithful, yet temperate history of Johnson, has been ably executed. In the succinct review of his writings, Mr. Murphy displays his own learning, judgment, and taste. His *Prayers and Meditations* were published from his manuscripts, by George Strahan, A. M. Vicar of Islington, in 8vo, 1785. *Letters to and from Samuel Johnson, LL. D.* were published by Mrs. Piozzi, in 2 vols. 8vo, 1788. The *Sermons* 8vo, 1790, left for publication, by Dr. Taylor, were unquestionably Johnson's ; and the fact is now ascertained on the authority of Mr. Hayes, the editor. An imperfect collection of his *Poems* was published by Kearsley, in 12mo, 1785 ; and inserted, with considerable additions, in the edition of " The Works of the English Poets," 1790. They are reprinted in the present collection, together with the tragedy of

Irene, and feveral additional pieces collected from Mr. Bofwell's " Life of Johnfon," and other publications.

The religious, moral, political, and literary character of Johnfon, will be better underftood by this account of his life, than by any laboured and critical comments. Yet it may not be fuperfluous here to attempt to collect, into one view, his moft prominent excellencies, and diftinguifhing particularities.

His figure and manner are more generally known than thofe of almoft any other man. His perfon was large, robuft, and unwieldy from corpulency. His carriage was disfigured by fudden emotions which appeared to a common obferver to be involuntary and convulfive. But in the opinion of Sir Jofhua Reynolds, they were the confequence of a depraved habit of accompanying his thoughts with certain untoward actions, which feemed as if they were meant to reprobate fome part of his paft conduct. Of his limbs, he is faid never to have enjoyed the free and vigorous ufe. When he walked, it feemed the ftruggling gait of one in fetters; and when he rode, he appeared to have no command over his horfe. His ftrength, however, was great, and his perfonal courage no lefs fo. A-mong other inftances, which exemplify his poffeffion of both, it is related, that, being once at the Litchfield theatre, he fat upon a chair placed for him befide the fcenes. Having had occafion to quit his feat, he found it occupied, upon his return, by an innkeeper of the town. He civilly demanded that it fhould be reftored to him; but meeting with a rude refufal, he laid hold of the chair, and with it, of the intruder, and flung them both, without further ceremony, into the pit. At another time, having engaged in a fcuffle with four men in the ftreet, he refolutely refufed to yield to fuperior numbers, and kept them all at bay, until the watch came up and carried him and his antagonifts to the watch-houfe. In his drefs he was fingular and flovenly; and though he improved fomewhat under the lectures of Mrs. Thrale, during his long refidence at Streatham, yet he was never able completely to furmount particularity. He never wore a watch till he was fixty years of age, and then caufed one to be made for him by Mudge and Dutton, which coft him feventeen guineas, with this infcription on the dial-plate, " For the night cometh." He was fond of good company, and of good living; and, to the laft, he knew of no method of regulating his appetites, but abfolute reftraint or unlimited indulgence. " Many a day," fays Mr. Bofwell, " did he faft; many a year refrain from wine: but when he did eat, it was voracioufly; when he did drink wine, it was copioufly. *He could practife abfti-*

nence, but not temperance." In converſation,
he was rude, intemperate, overbearing, and
impatient of contradiction. Addicted to
argument, and greedy of victory, he was
equally regardleſs of truth and fair reaſon-
ing in his approaches to conqueſt. " There
is no arguing with him," ſaid Goldſmith,
alluding to a ſpeech in one of Cibber's
plays; " for if his piſtol miſſes fire, he
knocks you down with the butt end of it."
In the early part of his life, he had been
too much depreſſed ; in his latter years, too
laviſhly indulged. His temper had at firſt
been ſoured by diſappointment and penu-
ry, and his petulance was afterwards flatter-
ed by univerſal ſubmiſſion. In his converſation and goodneſs of heart, his friends
met with a recompenſe for that ſubmiſſion
which the ſovereignty of his genius chal-
lenged, and his temper exacted from them
to the uttermoſt. To great powers, he
united a perpetual and ardent deſire to ex-

cel; and even in an argument on the most indifferent subject, he generally engaged with the whole force and energy of his great abilities. Of his converſation, it is true, all that has been retained by Mr. Bofwell, does not ſeem to be worth recording. Judging of it moſt favourably, it is not much diſtinguiſhed by the flaſhes of wit, or the ſtrokes of humour. Where he appears ſerious, we are not always ſure that he ſpeaks the ſentiments of his conviction. Mr. Bofwell allows that he often talked for victory, and ſometimes took up the weaker ſide, as the moſt ingenious things could be ſaid on it. Truth, and the ableſt defences of truth, are mixed with error, and the moſt ingenious gloſſes which ingenuity could invent, or addreſs enforce. Authors are exalted, or depreciated, as the moment of hilarity or gloom was connected with the ſubject, or as the opinion of the ſpeaker was adverſe; and the whole is given as the ſentiment of Johnson. But for the inferiority of his converſation, to our opinion of the man, he has himſelf made a prophetic apology, in his firſt interview with his biographer, who was deſtined to retail it. " People may be taken in once, who imagine that an author is greater in private life than another man. Uncommon parts require uncommon opportunities for their exertions."

-With theſe defects, there was, however, ſcarcely a virtue of which he was not in principle poſſeſſed. He was humane, charitable, affectionate, and generous. - His moſt intemperate ſallies were the effects of an irrritable habit ; he offended only to repent. To the warm and active benevolence of his heart, all his friends have borne teſtimony. " He had nothing," ſays Goldſmith, " of the bear, but his ſkin." Misfortune had only to form her claim, in order to found her right to the uſe of his purſe, or the exerciſe of his talents. His houſe was an aſylum for the unhappy, beyond what a regard to perſonal convenience would have allowed ; and his income was diſtributed in the ſupport of his inmates, to an extent greater than general prudence would have permitted. The moſt honourable teſtimony to his moral and ſocial character, is the cordial eſteem of his friends and acquaintances. - He was known by no man by whom his loſs was not regretted. : Another great feature of his mind, was the love of independence. While he felt the ſtrength of his own powers, he deſpiſed, except in one inſtance, pecuniary aid. His penſion has been often mentioned, and ſubjected him to ſevere imputations. But let thoſe, who, like Johnſon, had no patrimony, who were not always willing to labour, and felt the conſtant recurrence of neceſſities, reject, without an adequate reaſon, an independent income,

which left his fentiments free, and required neither the fervility of adulation, nor
the labours of fervice. It is not uncommon to fee a defire to be independent, de-
generate into avarice. Johnfon did not
feel it early, for his benevolence counteracted it ; but he declined going into Italy,
when worth 1500l. befides his penfion, becaufe of the expence ; and we fee the furly
dignity; which formerly fpurned at an obligation, relaxed, in his refufal of Dr. Brocklefby's affiftance, and Lord Thurlow's very
delicate offer of the fame kind. Some
little cenfure is due to him for his eafy
faith, occafioned by his political prejudices,
in the forgeries of Lauder. That he fhould
have appeared in public, in company with
this defamer of Milton, is to be lamented.
Yet his renunciation of all connection with
Lauder, when his forgeries were detected,
is only a proof of his having believed (a
common weaknefs of worthy minds), with-

out examination, not that he was an ac-
complice with the impoftor.

— If there is any one trait by which Johnfon's mind can be difcriminated, it is gigantic vigour.   In information and tafte he
was excelled.; but what he ferioufly attempted, he executed with that mafterly
original boldnefs, which leaves us to regret
his indolence, that he exerted himfelf only in the moment when his powers were
wanting, and relapfed again into his literary idlenefs.   He united in himfelf what feldom are united, a vigorous and excurfive
imagination, with a ftrong and fteady judgment.   His memory was remarkably tenacious, and his apprehenfion wonderfully
quick and accurate.   He was rather a man
of learning than of fcience.   He had accumulated a vaft fund of knowledge, without much of fyftem or methodical arrangement.   His reading feems to have been
cafual, generally defultory.   To converfa-

tion he owed much of his varied knowledge; and to his vigorous comprehenfive
powers, he was indebted for that clearnefs
of diftinction, that pointed judicious difcrimination, which elucidated every queftion,
and aftonifhed every hearer. From this
cafual reading, he rofe with a mind feldom
fatigued, endowed with a clear, accurate
perception; the variety of his ftudies relieved, without fatiguing or perplexing him;
the ideas arranged in order, were ready for
ufe, adorned with all the energy of language, and the force of manner. But the
labour of literature was a tafk from which
he always wifhed to efcape; and as he could
excel others without great exertion, we feldom perceive his faculties brought forward
in their full power. We fcarcely fee any
attempt, beyond a periodical paper, which
he did not profeffedly continue with laffi-
tude and fatigue.

He deferves the character of mafter of the Latin language; but it is eafy to perceive that his acquaintance with Greek literature was, what it is commonly fuppofed to be, general and fuperficial, rather than curious or profound. Of natural fcience he knew but little; and moft of his notions on that branch of philofophy were obfolete and erroneous. In his writings he appears to have taken more from his own mind than from books, and he difplays his learning rather in allufions to the opinions of others, than in the direct ufe of them. Hiftory he profeffed to difregard; yet his memory was fo tenacious, that we feldom find him at a lofs upon any topic, ancient or modern.

From early prejudices, which all his philofphy and learning could never overcome, he was a zealous and fcrupulous high-church-man, following to the uttermoft tenet, the notions of *Laud*, whofe talents

talents he has praifed, and whofe genius he has deplored in his *Vanity of Human Wifhes*. In his political fentiments, he was a rank Tory, and till his prefent Majefty's acceffion to the throne, a violent Jacobite. He had never examined either his religious or political creed. Bigotted as to a particular fyftem of politics, he appears obftinately to have clofed his eyes againft the light of truth; and fo far from feeking information on the fubject, ftudioufly refifted it. His piety was truly venerable and edifying. In divinity, however, his refearches were limited. He was well acquainted with the general evidences of Chriftianity; but he does not appear to have read his Bible with a critical eye, nor to have interefted himfelf concerning the elucidation of obfcure or difficult paffages. It was his favourite maxim, " that the proper ftudy of mankind is man ;" and we muft confefs that in all the departments of

moral fcience, his excellence is unrivalled.
His acute penetration was conftantly alive
to " catch the manners living as they rife,"
and but few follies or peculiarities could
efcape his obfervation.

The habitual weakneffes of his mind
form a ftriking and melancholy contraft to
the vigour of his underftanding. His opinions were tainted with prejudices almoft
too coarfe and childifh for the vulgar to
imbibe. His attachment to the univerfity
of Oxford, to which in his youth he owed
no great obligations, led him unjuftly to
depreciate the merit of every perfon who
had ftudied at that of Cambridge. - His
averfion to Whigs, Diffenters, and Prefby-
terians, and his diflike to Scotland, and
many more extravagancies of opinion, that
it would be painful to enumerate, inflamed
his converfation, and influenced his conduct. He was fo prone to fuperftition as

to make it a rule that a particular foot
fhould conftantly make the firft actual
movement, when he came clofe to the
threfhold of any door or paffage, which he
was about to enter, or to quit. So deeply
was he infected upon this fubject, that Mr.
Bofwell relates that he has often feen him
" when he had neglected or gone wrong
in this fort of magical movement, go back
again, put himfelf in a proper pofture to
begin the ceremony, and having gone
through it, break from his abftraction,
walk brifkly on, and join his companion."
He took off his hat in token of reverence,
when he approached the places on which
Popifh churches had formerly ftood ; and
bowed before the monaftic veftiges. He
was folicitous to give authenticity to ftories
of apparitions, and eager to credit the exiftence of a fecond-fight, while he appeared fcrupulous and fceptical as to particular facts. Thefe mental diftempers were

the offspring of his melancholic temperament, and were foftered by folitary contemplation, till they had laid fetters upon the imagination too ftrong for reafon to burft through. We fee it exerted in different circumftances, and expanding its gloomy influence, till at laft it terminated little fhort of infanity. To this ftate we muft attribute his mentioning fecret tranfgreffions, his conftant fear of death, and his religious terrors, not very confiftent with his ftrength of mind, or his conviction of the goodnefs of God. This, at leaft, feems to have been his own opinion of the progrefs of thefe difeafes, as appears from his hiftory of the *Mad Aftronomer* in *Raffelas*, the defcription of whofe mind he feems to have intended as a reprefentation of his own.

But let us turn from thefe foibles and fingularities, which fhow him weaker than the generality of his fellow men, and point to thofe perfections of mind, which prove him to have been of a rank fo much above them.

As an author, Johnson has diftinguifhed himfelf as a *philologift*, a *biographer*, a *critic*, a *moralift*, a *novelift*, a *political writer*, and a *poet*.

On his *Dictionary of the English Language*, it is unneceffary to enlarge. It is in every body's hands; its utility is univerfally ac-knowledged; and its popularity is its beft eulogium. The etymologies, though they exhibit learning and judgment, are not entitled to unqualified praife. The defi-nitions exhibit aftonifhing proofs of acute-nefs of intellect, and precifion of language. A few of them muft be admitted to be er-roneous. Thus, *Windward* and *Leeward*, though directly of oppofite meaning, are defined identically the fame way. The definition of *Net-work* has been often quot-ed with fportive malignity, as obfcuring

a thing in itfelf very plain. His introdu-
cing his own opinions, and even prejudices,
under general definitions of words, as *Tory*,
Whig, *Penfion*, *Oats*, *Excife*, and a few more,
muft be placed to the account of capricious and humourous indulgence. To his
lift of technical and provincial words, nine
thoufand have been added by Mr. Herbert
Croft, in his " Dictionary of the Englifh
Language;" the publication of which is
delayed for want of fuitable encouragement.

As a *biographer*, his merit is of the higheft kind. His narration in general is vigorous, connected, and perfpicuous; and
his reflections numerous, appofite, and moral. But it muft be owned that he neither
dwells with pleafure or fuccefs upon thofe
minuter anecdotes of life which oftener
fhow the genuine man, than actions of
greater importance. Sometimes, alfo, his
colourings receive a tinge from preju-

dice, and his judgment is infenfibly warp-
ed by the particularity of his private opinion. Thefe obfervations apply to his *Life
of Savage*, the moft finifhed of his biographical difquifitions; and his *Lives* of feveral other eminent men, which were originally printed in the " Gentleman's Magazine," and in other periodical publications,
and afterwards collected by Mr. Davies, in
his " Mifcellaneous and Fugitive Pieces,"
and to his *Lives of the Poets*.

As a *critic*, he is entitled to the praife of
being the greateft that our nation has produced. He has not, like his prodeceffors,
tried merely to learn the art, and not to
feel it. He has not gone to Dacier or to
Boffu, to borrow rules to fetter genius by
example, and impart diftinctions which
lead to no end; but, poffeffed of two qualities, without which a critic is no more
than a caviller, ftrong fenfe, and an intimate knowledge of human nature, he has

followed his own judgment, unbiaffed by authority, and has adopted all the good fenfe of Ariftotle, untrammelled by his forms. This praife he has merited by his *Preface to Shakfpeare*, and the detached pieces of criticifm which appear among his works. But his critical powers fhine with more concentrated radiance in the *Lives of the Poets*. Thefe compofitions, abounding in ftrong and juft illuftrations of criticifm, evince the vigour of his mind, and that happy art of moralization, by which he gives to well-known incidents the grace of novelty and the force of inftruction; and " grapples the attention," by expreffing common thoughts with uncommon ftrength and elegance. Of many paffages, it is fcarcely hyperbolical to affirm, that they are executed with all the fkill and penetration of Ariftotle, and animated and embellifhed with all the fire of Longinus. The *Lives* of *Cowley*, *Milton*,

Butler, *Waller*, *Dryden*, *Addison*, and *Pope*, are elaborately compofed, and exhibit the nobleft fpecimens of entertaining and folid criticifm, that ancient or modern times have produced. The differtation in the *Life of Cowley*, on the metaphyfical poets of the laft century, has all the attraction of novelty, as well as found obfervation. In the review of his works, falfe wit is detected in all its fhapes; and the Gothic tafte for glittering conceits, and far-fetched allufions, is exploded, never, it is hoped, to revive again. The " Paradife Loft," is a poem which the mind of *Milton* only could have produced; the criticifm upon it is fuch as, perhaps, the pen of Johnfon only could have written. His eftimate of *Dryden* and *Pope*, challenges Quintilian's remarks upon Demofthenes and Cicero, and rivals the fineft fpecimens of elegant compofition and critical acutenefs in the Englifh language. Some caution, however, is

required to perufe thefe admirable compofitions with advantage. The prefent
writer means not to fay that they are perfect, or that, on the whole, they are executed with propriety. If they be regarded merely as containing narrations of the
lives, delineations of the characters, and
ftrictures of the feveral authors, they are
far from being always to be depended upon. Johnfon, as he has had occafion to
remark, in reviewing his judgments of the
feveral poets who have fallen under his
confideration, brought to the production
of this work ideas already formed, opinions tinctured with his ufual hues of party
and prejudice, and the rigid unfeeling
philofophy, which could neither bend to
excufe failings, or judge of what was not
capable of a difpaffionate difquifition.

To think for himfelf in critical, as in all
other matters, is a privilege to which every
one is undoubtedly entitled. This privi-

lege of critical independence, an affectation of singularity, or some other principle
not immediately visible, is frequently be-
traying into a dogmatical spirit of contradiction to received opinion. Of this there
need no further proofs, than his almost
uniform attempt to depreciate the writers
of blank verse, and his degrading estimate
of the exquisite compositions of Prior,
Hammond, Collins, Gray, Shenstone, and
Akenside, and his pronouncing the " Pa-
radise Lost" " one of those books which
the reader admires and lays down, and forgets to take it up again." In his judgments of these poets, he may be justly ac-
cused of being inflamed by prejudice, re-
solutely blind to merit. His rigorous condemnation, and puerile criticisms upon
Gray, and his fastidious judgment of Shenstone, have drawn down upon him the united censures of those who admire poetry in
her most daring attitudes and gorgeous at-

tire, and those who are pleased with her modeft beauties, moft humble fteps, and leaft adorned guife. He obferves of Shen-ftone, that he fet little value upon thofe parts of knowledge which he had not cultivated himfelf. His own tafte of poetry feems in fome degree regulated by a fimilar ftandard; method, ratiocination, and argument, efpecially if the vehicle be rhyme, often obtaining his regard and commendation, while the bold and enthu-fiaftic, though perhaps irregular flights of imagination, are paffed by with obftinate and perverfe indifference. It is not, then, to be wondered at, that the panegyrift of Blackmore fhould withhold from Collins and Gray the commendation he has be-ftowed on Savage and Yalden; and that his praifes of the whole clafs of defcriptive poets are parfimonioufly beftowed, and too frigid to make an impreffion. This is to be attributed to the natural turn of his

mind, and to the bent which his feelings
had received from the habits of his life.
A certain inelegance of tafte, a frigid chur-
lifhnefs of temper, unfubdued and unqualified by that melting fenfibility, that divine enthufiafm of foul, which are effential to a hearty relifh of poetical compofition, too often counteracted and corrupt-
ed the other poetical virtues of his intellect. Poetry pleafes only as it is the image
of reality. He who has never delighted
in the filent beauties of creation, can feel
no emotions, as they are reflected to him
in defcription. Accuftomed to dogmatize
in his clofet, and fwelter in fome alley in
the city, Johnfon's mind never throbbed
with poetic thrills, as nature expanded her
rural glories to his eye; and he preferred
the duft of Fleet-Street, or the windings
of the Strand, to the air of Hampftead, or
the beauties of Greenwich.

One general remark may be ventured upon here: Through the whole of his work, the defire of praife, except in the cafe of fome very favourite author, is almoft always overpowered by his difpofition to cenfure; and while beauties are paffed over " with the neutrality of a ftranger, and the coldnefs of a critic," the flighteft blemifh is examined with microfcopical fagacity. The truth of this obfervation is particularly obvious, when he defcends to his contemporaries, for whom he appears to have little more brotherly kindnefs, than they might have expected at Conftantinople. The prefent writer is under no apprehenfion of being charged with an unjuftifiable partiality in this opinion of him, by thofe who know his difpofition and the habits of his life. All that is great and genuinely good in Johnfon, have had no warmer encomiaft. He has uniformly praifed his genius, his learn-

ing, his good fenfe, the ftrength of his reafonings, the fagacity of his critical decifions, the happinefs of his illuftrations, and
the animation and energy of his ftyle: He
has acknowledged that there is no fatiety
in the delight he infpires on moral and religious themes; and he makes no fcruple to
declare, that, though there are many opinions erroneous, and many obfervations im-
proper, a great part of his *Lives of the Poets*
is fuch as no one but himfelf could have
executed, and in which he will not be followed with fuccefs.

As a *moralift*, his periodical papers are
diftinguifhed from thofe of other writers,
who have derived celebrity from fimilar
publications. He has neither the wit nor
the graceful eafe of Addifon; nor does he
fhine with the humour and claffic fuavity
of Goldfmith. His powers are of a more
grave, energic, and dignified kind, than
any of his competitors; and if he enter-

tains us lefs, he inftructs us more. He
fhows himfelf mafter of all the receffes of
the human mind, able to detect vice, when
difguifed in her moft fpecious form, and
equally poffefled of a corrofive to eradicate,
or a lenitive to affuage the follies and for-
-rows of the heart. Virtuous in his object,
juft in his conceptions, ftrong in his arguments, and powerful in his exhortations,
he arrefts the attention of levity by the
luxuriance of his imagery, and grandilo-
quence of his diction; while he awes detected guilt into fubmiffion by the majefty of his declamation, and the fterling
weight of his opinions. But his genius is
only formed to chaftife graver faults, which
require to be touched with an heavier
hand. He could not chafe away fuch
lighter foibles as buzz in our ears in fociety, and fret the feelings of our lefs important hours. His gigantic powers were
able to prepare the immortal path to hea-

ven, but could not ftoop to decorate our manners with thefe leffer graces, which make life amiable. Johnfon, at fuch a tafk, was Hercules at the diftaff, a lion courfing of a moufe, or an eagle ftooping at a fly. He was formed to fuftain the character of a majeftic teacher of moral and religious wifdom. His *Rambler* furnifhes fuch an affemblage of difcourfes on practical religion and moral duty, of critical inveftigations, and allegorical and oriental tales, that no mind can be thought very deficient, that has by conftant ftudy and meditation affimilated to itfelf all that may be found there. Though inftruction be its predominant purpofe, yet it is enlivened with a confiderable portion of amufement. Nos. 19, 44, 82, 88, 179, 182, 194, 195, 197, and 198, may be appealed to for inftances of fertility of fancy, and accurate defcription of real life. Every page of the *Rambler* fhows a mind teem-

ing with claſſical alluſion and poetical imagery: illuſtrations from other writers, are
upon all occaſions ſo ready, and mingle ſo
eaſily in his periods, that the whole appears of one uniform vivid texture. The
ſerious papers in his *Idler*, though inferior
to thoſe in the Rambler, in ſublimity and
ſplendor, are diſtinguiſhed by the ſame
dignified morality and ſolemn philoſophy,
and lead to the ſame great end of diffuſing
wiſdom, virtue, and happineſs. The humourous papers are light and lively, and
more in the manner of Addiſon.

As a *noveliſt*, the amazing powers of his
imagination, and his unbounded knowledge of men and manners, may be plainly traced in the *oriental tales* in the *Rambler*, in which he has not only ſupported
to the utmoſt, the ſublimity of the eaſtern
manner of expreſſion, but even greatly
excelled any of the oriental writers, in the
fertility of his invention, the conduct of

his plots, and the juftnefs and ftrength of his fentiments. His capital work of that kind is his *Raffelas*. None of his writings have been fo extenfively diffufed over Europe. Such a reception demonftrates great beauties in the work; and there is no doubt that great beauties do exift there. The language enchants us with harmony; the arguments are acute and ingenious; the reflections novel, yet juft. It aftonifhes with the fublimity of its fentiments, and at the fertility of its illuftrations, and delights with the abundance and propriety of its imagery. The fund of thinking which it contains, is fuch, that almoft every fentence of it may furnifh a fubject of long meditation. But it is not without its faults. It is barren of interefting incidents, and deftitute of originality, or diftinction of characters. There is little difference in the manner of thinking and reafoning of the philofopher and the fe-

male, of the prince and the waiting woman. *Nekagah* and *Imlac*, *Raffelas* and
Pekuah, are all equally argumentative, ab-
ftracted, eloquent, and obftinate. Of that
dark catalogue of calamities, which are
defcribed as incident to the feveral fituations of life which he contemplates, fome
are not the neceffary confequence of the
fituation, but of the temper; and others
are not thofe which are moft generally or
feverely felt there. The moral that he
feeks to inculcate, that there is no fuch
thing as happinefs, is one ungrateful to
the human heart. If he could fucceed in
eftablifhing it, it would cripple every in-
citement to virtue, and palfy every fti-
mulus to action. It would leave man con-
tented to be drifted down the ftream of
life, without an object or an end; to lofe
attainable excellence for the want of exertion, and fink under furmountable difficulties, without a ftruggle. Though there

may not be permanent happine∫s in the gratification of our wi∫hes, there is much in our expectations that they will be gratified. Hope is the ∫weet and innocent ∫olace of our frail natures. It is the ∫taff of the unhappy, and however feeble its ∫upport, it is immoral and unkind to wre∫t it from our hands.

The effect of *Ra∬elas*, and of John∫on's other moral *tales*, is thus beautifully illu∫trated by Mr. Courtenay, in his " Poetical Review ;"

> Impre∬ive truth, in ∫plendid fiction dre∫t,
> Checks the vain wi∫h, and calms the troubled brea∫t ;
> O'er the dark mind a light cele∫tial throws,
> And ∫ooths the angry pa∬ions to repo∫e.
> As oil effus'd illumes and ∫mooths the deep,
> When round the bark the ∫welling ∫urges ∫weep.

As a *political writer*, his productions are more di∫tingui∫hed by ∫ubtlety of di∫qui∫ition, poignancy of ∫arca∫m, and dignity and energy of ∫tyle, than by truth, equity, or candour. He makes much more u∫e of his rhetoric than of his logic, and often gives his reader high-founding declamation inftead of fair argument. In perufing his reprefentations of thofe who differed from him on political fubjects, we are fometimes inclined to affent to a propofition of his own, that " there is no credit due to a rhetorician's account, either of good or evil." Many pofitions are laid down in admirable language, and in highly-polifhed periods, which are inconfiftent with the principles of the Britifh conftitution, and repugnant to the common rights of mankind. It muft always be regretted, that a man of Johnfon's intellectual powers, fhould have had fo ftrong a propenfity to defend arbitrary principles of government. But, on this fubject, the ftrength of his language was not more manifeft, than the weaknefs of his arguments. In apology for him, it may be admitted, that he was a Tory from principle, and that moſt of what he wrote, was conformable to his real ſentiments. But to defend all that was written by him, his warmeſt friends will find impoſſible.

In his poſthumous writings, there is little that can be ſaid to be intereſting to ſcience or criticiſm. His *Letters* are valuable, as we find in them the picture, which, without intending it, he has left of himſelf, to be that of a man, who, to great intellectual powers, added extraordinary piety, and many excellent moral qualities. Of letter writing, he gives his idea in the following paſſage: " Some, when they write to their friends, are all affection; ſome are wiſe and ſententious; ſome ſtrain their powers for effects of gravity; ſome write news; and ſome write ſecrets; but to make a letter without affection, without wiſdom, without gravity, without news, and without ſecrets, is doubtleſs the great epiſtolic ſtyle. There is a pleaſure

in corresponding with a friend, where
doubt and mistrust have no place, and e-
very thing is said as it is thought. These
are the letters by which souls are united,
and by which minds, naturally in unison,
move each other, as they are moved them-
selves. Let me know where you are, how
you got thither, how you live there? and
every thing that one friend loves to know
of another." Such is the account of his
Letters. The value of them is, that we
have the man before us for near twenty
years. We see him in his undress, that
is, the undress of his mind, which, unlike
that of his body, was never slovenly. We
see him in health and in sickness, and in
all the petty business of life. From himself, and in his own words, we are enabled
to collect the truest and best information.
He writes always in his own style. His
words are now and then too pompous for
familiar letters ; but his skill in letter writ-

ing comes out fully in this collection, and entitles him to rank with the best epistolary writers of our nation. His letters on the death of Mrs. Salusbury (mother of Mrs. Piozzi), and Mr. Thrale's eldest son, are at once moral and pathetic. They flow from a man, who loved them, and the surviving family. His solicitude for Mr. Thrale, during a long illness, and his feelings at his death, do honour to the memory of Mr. Thrale, and to Johnson's gratitude and sensibility. "I am afraid," he says, "of thinking what I have lost: I never had such a friend before." To Mrs. Thrale, he says, "To see and hear you, is always to hear wit and see virtue." He seems at times to think her regard for him is abated; and a letter of kindness from her appears to have revived and comforted him. After lamenting the loss of Williams and Levett, he says: "Such society I had with them, and such I had

———where I am never likely to have it more." When I came to " love and honour," in your letter, I said to myself, " How lov'd, how honour'd once, avails me not." Shall we never again exchange our thoughts by the firefide ?" After feeing him ftruggle with illnefs and morbid melancholy, it is comfortable to hear him fay, almoft at the clofe of life " Attention and refpect give pleafure, however late, and however ufelefs. But they are not ufelefs, even when they are late ; it is reafonable to rejoice as the day declines, to find that it has been fpent with the approbation of mankind."

His *Prayers and Meditations*, publifhed by Mr. Strahan, " at his own requeft," have occafioned much concern, difquietude, and offence in the minds of many, who apprehend that the caufe in which he ftood forth, will fuffer by the infirmities of the advocate being expofed in this publication, to the prying and malignant eye of the world. It is not merely the name of Johnfon that is to do fervice to any caufe. His admirable arguments in favour of religion and morality, are not weakened by the proofs of his practical errors. Thefe are always precifely what they were, once good, and always good. His arguments in favour of felf-denial do not lofe their force *becaufe he fafted*, nor thofe in favour of devotion, *becaufe he faid his prayers.* His fafting and his prayers add ftrength to his pious reafonings, from the proof they afford, that he believed in the religion he inculcated. Human nature is frail; common frailties muft inevitably preclude perfection to the leaft faulty profeffor of Chriftianity. The world never fuppofed Johnfon to have been a perfect character. His ftupendous abilities, and great learning, it is well known, could not preferve their poffeffor from the depredations of melancholy. But his failings leaned to the fide of virtue. His fuperfti-tion feems to have arifen from the moft amiable difpofition in the world, " a pious awe, and fear to have offended," a wifh rather to do too much than too little. Such a difpofition one loves, and always wifhes to find in a friend; and it cannot be difagreeable in the fight of him who made us. It argues a fenfibility of heart, a tendernefs of confcience, and the fear of God. That he fhould not be confcious of the abilities with which Providence had bleffed him, was impoffible. He felt his own powers; he felt what he was capable of having performed, and he faw how little, comparatively fpeaking, he had performed. Hence his apprehenfions on the near profpect of the account to be made, viewed through the medium of conftitutional and morbid melancholy, which often excluded from his fight the bright

beams of divine mercy. His felf-abafe-
ment was ftrictly ingenuous; but his expreffions, when compared with the tenor
of his conduct, feem too difparaging.
Chriftianity does not require us to deny
any one quality we poffefs, or to reprefent
ourfelves, in defiance of truth, as one mafs
of deformity and guilt. The inftruction
of St. Paul, enforced by the moft facred
example, is fingly this, that we " think
not of ourfelves more highly than we ought
to think; but that we think foberly."
Johnfon walked at all times humbly with
his God; but when we follow him through
all his weakneffes, his religious horrors,
and facred punctilios, we are inclined to
pity the conftitutional feeblenefs of his
nature, while we admire the perfeverance
and fervour of his devotion. We owe to
the excellencies of the Supreme Being,
every poffible degree of veneration and
honour; but that virtue fhould tremble in

the prefence of Infinite Goodnefs, is not lefs contrary to reafon, than it is contrary to heroifm. In the prefence of Infinite Goodnefs it feels a congeniality, and af-fumes a confidence, that leaps, as it were, the gulf between, and dares to afpire to fentiments of attachment, fidelity and love. But it would be unfair to conclude from this circumftance, that the piety and hu-mility of Johnfon were of no value; and the fincerity of his repentance, the fted-faftnefs of his faith, and the fervour of his charity, of no ufe. There is fomething fo great and awful in the idea of a God, and fomething fo fafcinating in the effufions of gratitude, that there are numbers of men intrepid and heroical, in every other re-gard, that cannot boaft of all the ferenity and affurance in the bufinefs of religion, that are fo earneftly to be defired; and yet the piety of thefe men is edifying and venerable. Indeed the fate of " the un-

profitable fervant" may juftly beget apprehenfions in the ftouteft mind. - Language
affords no finer expreffions than thofe in
which the *Prayers* of Johnfon are conceived. They are fhort, fimple, and unadorn-
ed. - They bear fome refemblance to the
Collects in the " Common Prayer-Book,"
without that dignity which is derived to
the latter, from the venerable antiquity of
the ftyle and expreffion. They have no
particular method, no difplay of genius,
and no beauties that fhould characterize
the man under whofe name they appear.
- They have nothing that might not have
been produced by any man of plain common fenfe. At the fame time they contain few traces of weaknefs or abfurdity.
Never did there exift a greater difparity
between the performances of the fame author, than between this publication and
the *Lives of the Poets*, or the numbers of the
Rambler. His *Meditations*, as they are im-

properly called, are merely minutes; at one time of refolutions for his future conduct; and at another, in the ftyle of a diary or journal. Neither of them deferve the commendation which has been beftowed upon the *Prayers*. They are full of frivolous minuteneffes, and feminine weaknefs, beyond any thing of which an abftract defcription can fuggeft the idea. They tell us, that Johnfon, in fpite of all the contemptuous ridicule with which he has treated that delicate frame, which depends for its compofure on the clouds and the winds, was himfelf not exempt from languor, fluggifhnefs, and procraftination; that he was full of the moft pitiable religious credulity; and that his attention was often engroffed by things in the laft degree frivolous, futile, and unimportant. But if thefe obfervations are rather difadvantageous to Johnfon, it is no lefs unqueftionable that he difplays a fenfibility and a humane benovolence of heart, that have rarely been equalled. Mr. Strahan's apology for Johnfon's *feeming* to pray for his deceafed wife, is fupported by his opinion, refpecting purgatory, recorded by Mr. Bofwell. In his cooler moments he did not think fuch prayers proper, except with the limitations there expreffed; but his morbid melancholy did not always allow him to be cool; there were many moments when his language countenanced a very different opinion. The ftruggle in a breaft, conftituted as his was, between the fevere principles of Proteftantifm, and the genuine undifciplinable feelings of the heart, illuftrates the kindnefs of his nature more than it could be illuftrated by any other circumftance.

His *Sermons*, publifhed under the name of *Dr. Taylor*, are not unworthy of the author of the *Rambler*, and afford additional proof of his ardour in the caufe of

piety, and every moral duty. The laſt
diſcourſe in the collection was intended
to be delivered by Dr. Taylor, at the funeral of Johnſon's wife, but he declined
the office, becauſe, as he told Mr. Hayes,
the praiſe of the deceaſed was too much
amplified. He who reads the diſcourſe,
will find it a beautiful moral leſſon, written with temper, and no where overcharged with ambitious ornaments. The reſt
of the diſcourſes were the fund which Dr.
Taylor, from time to time, carried with
him to the pulpit.

The *ſtyle* of his proſe writings has been
too often criticiſed, to need being noticed
here. It has been cenſured, applauded,
and imitated, to extremes equally dangerous to the purity of the Engliſh tongue.
That he has innovated upon our language
by his adoption of Latin derivatives and
his preference of abſtract to concrete terms,
cannot be denied. But the danger from

his innovation would be trifling, if thofe
alone would copy him who can think with
equal precifion ; for few paffages can be
pointed out from his works, in which
his meaning could be as accurately expreffed by fuch words as are in more
familiar ufe. His comprehenfion of mind
was the mould for his language. Had
his comprehenfion been narrower, his
expreffion would have been eafier. His
fentences have a dignified march, fuitable to the elevation of his fentiments,
and the pomp of his fonorous phrafeology.
And it is to be remembered, that while
he has added harmony and dignity to our
language, he has neither vitiated it by the
infertion of foreign idioms, or the affectation of anomaly in the conftruction of his
fentences. While the flowers of poetic
imagination luxuriantly adorn his ftyle, it
is never enfeebled by their plentitude. It
is clofe without obtenebration, perfpicuous
without languor, and ftrong without im-

petuofity. No periods are fo harmonious; none fo nervous. He has laboured his ftyle with the greateft attention ; perhaps its e-laboratenefs is too apparent. It has, per-haps, too unwieldy and too uniform a dignity. He feems to have been particularly ftudious of the glitter of an antithe-fis between the epithet and the fubftantive. This ftrikes while it is new ; but to the more experienced reader, though it may feem fometimes forcible, yet it will often prove tirefome. It is remarkable that Johnfon's early performances bear few marks of the ftyle which he adopted in his *Rambler*. In his *Life of Savage*, the ftyle is elegant, but not oftentatious. His fentences are naturally arranged, and mufical without artifice. He affects not the meafuring of claufes, and the balancing of periods. He aims not at fplendid, glowing diction. He feeks not pointed phrafes, and elaborate contrafts. It is alfo worthy of remark, on this fubject, that Johnfon has altered, and perhaps improved his ftyle, long after his reputation had been eftablifhed, and his *Rambler* had appeared. The compofition of this work differs a good deal from that of *Raffelas*, the *Journey to the Weftern Iflands*, and *The Lives of the Poets*. The native vigour, and peculiarity of feature, are indeed preferved, but they are polifhed to greater elegance, and taught to wear the appearance of a happier eafe. In the *Rambler* his periods are longer, and his meaning more condenfed; he is more fond of abftract terms, and ambitious of fefquipedalian words. But this work was written while he was occupied in collecting authorities for his *Dictionary*; at a time when Browne and Hooker, Bacon and Hakewell, were continually before him; men whom it was difficult to read, and remain free from the temptation to imitate. In his latter productions, particularly his *Lives of the Poets*, his fentences are fhorter, their conftruction more fimple, and the ufe of Latin derivations lefs frequent. He has made his ftyle in a greater degree elegant without conftraint, dignified without ambitious ornament, ftrong without rigidity, and harmonious without elaboration. He has adopted a meafured paufe, and a correfpondent length in the numbers of his periods, which gives to his profe much of the harmony, and fometimes fomewhat of the monotony of verfe. As Homer gave a peculiar language to his gods, to exprefs their divine conceptions, let us allow to Johnfon, and to men like him, a ftyle fuch as he has ufed; for we have as yet found none more grand and energetic. It is certain that his example has given a general elevation to the language of his country; for many of our beft writers have approached very near to him; and from the influence which he has had upon our compolition, scarcely any thing is written now, that is not better expreſſed than was uſual before he appeared to lead the national taſte. This circumſtance is well deſcribed by Mr. Courtenay, in his " Poetical Re-view ;" a performance which ſhows that he has caught no mean degree of the expan-ſion and harmony which characterize the ſtyle of Johnſon.

> By nature's gifts ordain'd mankind to rule, -
> He like a Titian form'd his brilliant ſchool,
> And taught congenial ſpirits to excel,
> While from his lips impreſſive wiſdom fell.

Among the congenial ſpirits " who formed the ſchool of Johnſon," Mr. Cour-tenay celebrates the reſpectable names of Goldſmith, Sir Joſhua Reynolds, Dr. Bur-ney, Mr. Malone, Mr. Steevens, Dr. Hawkeſ-worth, Sir William Jones, and Mr. Boſwell, and concludes his deſcription in the fol-lowing animated lines :

Nor was his energy confin'd alone
To friends around his philofophic throne;
His influence wide improv'd our letter'd ifle,
And lucid vigour mark'd the general ftyle;
As Nile's proud waves, fwoln from their oozy bed,
Firft o'er the neighb'ring mead majeftic fpread,
Till, gathering force, they more and more expand,
And with due virtue fertilize the land.

Among the imitators of Johnfon's ftyle, whether intentionally, or by the imperceptible effect of its ftrength and animation, may be reckoned a great proportion of the moft diftinguifhed writers in our language fince he appeared, Dr. Robertfon, Dr. Blair, Mr. Gibbon, Dr. Leland, Dr. Fergufon, Dr. Knox, Dr. Stuart, Dr. Parr, Dr. Thomfon, Dr. Gillies, Mr. Mackenzie, and Mr. Chalmers, &c. Perhaps the moft perfect imitation of Johnfon is a profeffed one, intituled " A Criticifm on Gray's Elegy in a Country Church-Yard," faid to be written by Dr. Young, Profeffor of Greek at Glafgow. It has not only the peculiarities of Johnſon's ſtyle, but that very ſpecies of literary diſcuſſion and illuſtration for which he was eminent.—But let men of moderate conceptions beware of ill judged imitations. Their attempt to copy his language is Salmoneus thundering at Elis, or a mortal wielding the ſpear of Pelides. It is to raiſe a melancholy contraſt between the ſlimneſs of the thought, and the capacity of the expreſſion, to cover the head of a pigmy with the caſque of a giant.

As a *poet*, the merit of Johnſon, though conſiderable, yet falls far ſhort of that which he has diſplayed in thoſe provinces of literature in which we have already ſurveyed him. As far as ſtrength of expreſſion, fruitfulneſs of invention, and abundance of imagery, conſtitute poetry, he is much more of a poet in his proſe works, than in his metrical compoſitions. Metaphor, to the merit of which he was blind and uncharitable, is ſo much the ſoul and

effence of poetry, that without it rhyme
and metre are vain. There may be fmoothnefs, fyllabic arrangement, and good fenfe,
in a metrical production ; but there can be
no true poetry without imagery, warm expreffion, and an enthufiafm which in-
toxicates the reader, lifts him above the
ground, and makes him forget that he is
mortal. Poetry is paffion; paffion is a temporary phrenzy, during which we both
hear and fee what we are totally infenfible
to in our fober fenfes. What did the an-
cients mean by the Pythian prieftefs being
numine afflata, when fhe received infpira-
tion, and delivered it in verfe, and in applying the fame idea to poets, but that they
had fuch a temporary delirium ? Ratiocination prevailed in Johnfon much more
than fenfibility. He has no daring fu-
blimities, nor gentle graces; he never glows
with the enthufiafm of the god, or kindles
a fympathetic emotion in the bofom of his

readers. His poems are the plain and fenfible effufions of a mind never hurried beyond itfelf, to which the ufe of rhyme
adds no beauty, and from which the ufe
of profe would detract no force. His
verfification is fmooth, flowing, and unreftrained; but his paufes are not fufficiently varied, to refcue him from the im-
putation of monotony. He feems never at
a lofs for rhyme, or deftitute of a proper
expreffion; and the manner of his verfe
appears admirably adapted to didactic or
fatiric poetry, for which his powers were
equally, and perhaps alone qualified.

His tragedy of *Irene* may be confidered
as the greateft effort of his genius. It is a
legitimate dramatic compofition. The u-
nities of time, place, and action, are ftrictly obferved. The diction is nervous, rich,
and elegant; but fplendid language, and
melodious numbers, will make a fine poem,
not a tragedy. The fubftance of the ftory

is fhortly this. In 1453, Mahomet the Great, firft emperor of the Turks, laid fiege to Conftantinople, and having reduced the place, became enamoured of a fair Greek, whofe name was *Irene.* The fultan invited her to embrace the law of Mahomet, and to grace his throne. Enraged at this intended marriage, the janizaries formed a confpiracy to dethrone the emperor. To avert the impending danger, Mahomet, in a full affembly of the grandees, " catching with one hand," as Knolles expreffes it, " the fair Greek by the hair of her head, and drawing his faulchion with the other, he, at one blow, ftruck off her head, to the great terror of them all ; and having fo done, faid unto them, " Now, by this, judge whether your emperor is able to bridle his affections or not." The ftory is fimple, and it remained for Johnfon to amplify it with proper epifodes, and give it complication and variety. But he has altered the character and cataftrophe, which he found in the hiftorian, fo as to diminifh the dramatic effect. Many faults may be found with the conduct of the fable. The principal one is, that the plot is double, and has the moft ftriking faults of fuch a fable; for it divides the fpectator's attention and regard between characters, whofe interefts are oppofite, and whofe happinefs or mifery is made to depend upon the fame events. We cannot hope the efcape of *Demetrius* and *Afpafia*, without dreading the condemnation of *Irene*; and our wifhes as to each, operating in contradiction, muft diminifh our concern for both. The cataftrophe, which is made to depend upon the fate of *Irene*, is meanly worked up. It is brought about too fuddenly, without a due connection with preparatory incidents, and at the very moment when we have not leifure to contemplate it, and are alone interefted for the efcape of *Demetrius* and *Af-*

pafia. We neither anticipate it with fufficient perfpicuity, nor confider it with folemnity, fo as to be affected, upon its occurrence, with genuine dramatic grief or terror. The characters of the piece have nothing difcriminative. They are not reprefentations of different tempers, paffions, and minds, but of different degrees of virtue and vice. They are fo naked of peculiarity, that we cannot know why the fame incidents fhould operate differently upon any one of them, fo as to impel them to a different action, or produce an emotion even varying in ftrength from what it would have done in any other. They poffefs too much of a balanced importance in the conduct of the drama, fo that the mind knows not how to make its election of a principal character, or to fix its attention upon any perfonage to whofe felicity it may attach its wifhes, and upon whofe fate it may fufpend its fympathy. From the name of the tragedy, we muſt ſuppoſe that Johnſon conſidered *Irene* as the *heroine*, yet the reader feels more concern, even for the ſtoic virtue and cool fondneſs of *Aſpaſia*. The former is too much of a mixed charaƈter; neither her goodneſs, nor her weakneſs, nor her depravity are predominant. She has not ſufficient virtue to awaken our ſympathy for the ſufferings of innocence, nor ſufficient vice to arouſe our terror at the puniſhment of guilt. The ſpeeches are oftener the recolleƈtions of paſt feelings, than the ebullitions of immediate paſſions, ſtarted by the paſſing aƈtions of the ſcene. Little is made preſent to the ſpeƈtator's mind, and of that little, nothing has life. His critique upon the tragic poets, of the commencement of this century, is, perhaps, in no inſtance, more true than it is of himſelf.

> From bard to bard the frigid caution crept,
> And declamation roar'd whilſt paſſion ſlept;

'Yet ſtill did virtue deign the ſtage to tread,
Philoſophy remain'd, though nature fled.

He has nothing of the fire of Lee, or the pathos of Otway. He is more declamatory than Rowe, and *Irene*, if poſſible, is colder than " Cato." There is not, throughout the play, a ſingle ſituation to excite curioſity, and raiſe a conflict of paſſions: The ſentiments are juſt and always moral, but ſeldom appropriated to the character, and generally too philoſophic. His poetical imagery is neither ſtriking nor abundant. The language in which the thoughts are conveyed, is, in general, vigorous, accurately poliſhed, and regularly muſical. It would be difficult to ſelect a paſſage in dramatic poetry more nobly conceived, or finely expreſſed, than the reply of *Demetrius* to the complaint of his friend, that no prodigy from Heaven had foretold the calamities of Greece.

Q

A thoufand horrid prodigies foretold it;
A feeble government, eluded laws,
A factious populace, luxurious nobles,
And all the maladies of finking ftates.
When public villany, too ftrong for juftice,
Shows his bold front, the harbinger of ruin,
Can brave Leontius call for any wonders,
Which cheats interpret, and which fools regard?
When fome neglected fabric nods beneath
The weight of years, and totters to the tempeft,
Muft Heaven difpatch the meffengers of light,
Or wake the dead to warn us of its fall?

As an alloy to the beauties of this paffage, impartial criticifm is compelled to
turn to another, which is furely little fhort
of nonfenfe, and well worthy of a place in
the treatife of " Scriblerus."

Oft have I rag'd, when their wide-wafting cannon
Lay pointed at our batteries, *yet unform'd*,
And *broke* the *meditated lines* of war.

Irene may be added to fome other plays
in our language, which have loft their
place in the theatre, but continue to pleafe
in the clofet. As it is the drama of our

great Englifh moralift; the prefent writer
fhould wifh to fee it revived:

Of the poetical compofitions, which are
known to be of his writing, the *Imitations
of Juvenal* are the beft ; and are, perhaps,
the nobleft imitations to be found in any
language. They are not fo clofe as thofe
done by Pope from Horace, but they are
infinitely more fpirited and energetic. In
.Pope, the moft peculiar images of Roman
life are adapted with fingular addrefs to
our own times ; in Johnfon; the fimilitude
is only in general paffages, fuitable to e-
very age in which refinement has degene-
rated into depravity.

His *London* breathes the true vehement
contemptuous indignation of Juvenal's fatire. It is more popular in its fubject, and
more animated in its compofition, than his
Vanity of Human Wifhes. It blazes forth
with the genuine fire of poetry, in the
livelinefs of its correfpondent allufions, the

energy of its expreſſions, and the frequen-
cy of its apoſtrophes. The *Vanity of Human Wiſhes* is more grave, moral, ſententious, and ſtately. In his *London* he often
takes nothing more than the ſubject from
the Roman poet, proves or illuſtrates it according to the originality of his own conceptions, or the warmth of his own fancy;
and ſometimes, too, he deſerts him altogether, and that not only where the modeſty of an Engliſh ear, and the inappli-
cability of the original to modern cuſtoms
require it, but in places where the topics
and the moral uſe is as applicable to London as they are to ancient Rome. Thus
he has either totally neglected, or but
ſlightly imitated that beautiful paſſage beginning at ver. 137.

> Dat teſtem Romæ tam ſanctum, quam fuit hoſpes
> Numinis Idæi, &c.

and ending with ver. 190,

—————præftare tributa clientes
Cogimur, et cultis augere peculia fervis.

The *Vanity of Human Wifhes* follows the original more clofely, but ftill with many omiffions. The fubject is taken from the fecond " Alcibiades" of Plato, and has an intermixture of the fentiments of Socrates, concerning the object of prayers offered up to the Deity. The general propofition is, that good and evil are fo little underftood by mankind, that their wifhes, when granted, are always deftructive. This is exemplified in a variety of inftances; fuch as riches, ftate-preferment, eloquence, military glory, long life, and the advantages of beauty. Juvenal's conclufion is admirable. " Let us," he fays, " leave it to the gods to judge what is fitteft for us. Man is dearer to his Creator than to himfelf. If we muft pray for any fpecial grace, let it be for a found mind, in a found body. Let us pray for fortitude,

that we may think the labours of Hercules, and all his fufferings, preferable to a
life of luxury, diffipation, and the foft re-
pofe of Sardanapulus. This is a bleffing
within the reach of every man; this we
can give ourfelves. It is virtue, and virtue only, that can make us happy. For
the characters which Juvenal has chofen
to illuftrate his doctrine, Johnfon has fub-
ftituted others from modern hiftory; for
Sejanus, he gives Cardinal *Wolfey*, *Buckingham*, ftabbed by Felton, *Strafford* and *Cla-
rendon*; for Demofthenes and Cicero, *Ly-
diat*, *Galileo*, and *Laud*; for Hannibal,
Charles XII; and to fhow the confequen-
ces of long life, he fays,

From *Marlb'rough's* eyes the ftreams of dotage flow,
And *Swift* expires a driveller and a fhow:

And of beauty he fays,

Yet *Vane* would tell what ills from beauty fpring,
And *Sedley* curs'd the form that pleas'd a king.

This laſt example is ill choſen ; for it is well known that the Counteſs of Dorcheſter, miſtreſs to James II. was not handſome. Owing to the dearth of modern examples, his inſtances are leſs numerous and leſs ſtriking than thoſe of Juvenal. His thoughts are not ſo compreſſed in the expreſſion, or ſo energetically conveyed to the mind, as thoſe of the Roman ſatiriſt ; but his diction is leſs laboured and affected, and he flows in a ſtream of verſification ſcarcely leſs rapid and eloquent, but infinitely more ſmooth than the Latin poet. He has preſerved all the beauties and virtue of the original moral, but ſtripped it, with infinite art, from all appearance of Epicuréan infidelity, and filled it with precepts worthy of a philoſopher, and wiſhes fitting for a Chriſtian. He has ſucceeded wonderfully in giving to his imitation the air of an original. The Chriſtian had to ſtruggle with the Heathen

poet, and though we cannot fay that he
has furpaffed him, he has, at leaft, entered into a noble competition.

Of his fmaller poems, the *Prologue for
the Opening of Drury-Lane Theatre*, has been
univerfally admired, as a mafterly and
comprehenfive criticifm upon the feveral
ages of Englifh dramatic poetry. The
fubject and the moral were well conceived,
and are as nobly expreffed. The character of *Shakfpeare* is delineated with a felicity of expreffion, that challenges the
whole compafs of Englifh poetry. His
other *Prologues* are copies of his mind,
clear and comprehenfive, pointed and e-
nergetic. Of his *Odes* upon the feafons,
his addreffes to *Autumn* and *Winter* feem
the beft. Many of the ftanzas are exceedingly beautiful; as ufual, moral, and un-
ufually pathetic. They manifeft, however, that his defcriptive poetry is not the
production of a warm fancy, impelled to

give vent by poefy to its overflowing feelings. Thofe paffions and objects which would infpire the genuine poetic mind with enthufiafm, pafs by him unfelt and unnoticed. He is melancholy in Spring, jocund in Winter; he lavifhes no encomiums upon the perfumed zephyrs, but flies to melancholy morals, or commemorates the comforts of a cheering flaggon and a fnug fire-fide. His *Ode to Evening*, addreffed to *Stella*, the *Natural Beauty*, and the *Vanity of Wealth*, are in general elegant. The firft is warm and fentimental, and fhows that he was neither ignorant of the feelings, nor infenfible to the joys of a lover. The *Ode to Friendfhip* is diftinguifhed by delicacy of fentiment and beauty of expreffion. Of his addrefs *To Lyce*, the idea perhaps is not original; but the images are happily felected, and well exprefled. *Stella in Mourning*, the verfes to *Lady Firebrace, To an elderly Lady*, and *On the Sprig of Myrtle*, are occasional compositions, and of course derive their merit chiefly from local and temporary circumstances. The principal art in such performances, is to make a trifling circumstance poetical or witty. In the verses *On the Sprig of Myrtle*, he has very happily succeeded. The *Ant* must be allowed to be nervous and elegant. The verses *On the Death of Stephen Grey*, are worthy the pen of Pope.

The *Elegy on the Death of Mr. Levett*, as it was among the last, so it is one of the best of his performances. It is moral, characteristic, and pathetic. The following stanzas are exquisitely beautiful.

> Yet still he fills affection's eye,
>   Obscurely wise and coarsely kind ;
> Nor letter'd arrogance deny
>   This praise to merit unrefin'd.
> When fainting nature call'd for aid,
>   And hovering death prepar'd the blow,
> His vigorous remedy display'd
>   The power of art without the show :

In mifery's darkeft cavern known,
  His ufeful care was ever nigh,
Where hopelefs anguifh pour'd his groan,
  And lonely want retir'd to die.
No fummons mock'd by chill delay,
  No petty gain difdain'd by pride;
The modeft wants of every day
  The toil of every day fupply'd.

The concluding lines are exceptionable:

Death broke at once the *vital chain*,
  And forc'd his foul the *neareft way*.

Since it is the foul which gives *life*, the chain that confines the foul is coporeal: The *vital* chain cannot be faid, with propriety, to be broken by death. Johnfon would not have forgiven an error of this kind in Gray.

Of his remaining pieces, fome are mere impromptus, which were never intended for the public eye, and others were the fuggeftions of temporary incidents. Many of them are fprightly and elegant, and may be read with pleafure; but they require no diſtinct enumeration, or particular criticiſm.

Among our Engliſh poets, it is no unpleaſant reflection to be able to find ſo many elegant writers of Latin verſe; in the firſt rank of which, Johnſon ſtands very high. Jonſon, Craſhaw, Cowley, May, Milton, Marvel, Addiſon, Gray, Smart, Warton, and Johnſon, are ſuch writers of Latin verſe, as any country might with juſtice be proud to own. Johnſon was eminently ſkilled in the Latin tongue, and ſtrongly attached to the cultivation of Latin poetry. The firſt fruits of his genius were compoſitions in Latin verſe. His tranſlation of the *Meſſiah*, gained him reputation in the college in which it was written, and was approved by Pope. Virgil ſeems to have been his model for language and verſification. He has copied the varied pauſes of his verſe, the length of his periods, the peculiar grace of his expreffions, and his majeftic dignity, with confiderable fuccefs. But his compofition is fometimes unclaffical and incorrect. The moft exceptionable line is the firft; *tollere concentum*, if allowable, is furely an awkward phrafe for " begin the fong." His *Odes*, particularly, the *Ode Inchkenneth*, *Ode in the Ifle of Sky*, and that *to Mrs. Thrale*, from the fame place, are eafy, elegant, and poetical. They unite claffical language, tender fentiment, and harmonious verfe. His poem, Γνῶθι σεαυτον, is nervous and energetic. His *Epitaphs* are diftinguifhed by claffical elegance and nervous fimplicity. Thofe on *Goldfmith* and *Thrale* feem the beft. His *Epigrams* are, in general, neat and pointed. In the *Anthologia*, we admire fometimes a happy imitation, and fometimes regret inelegant expreffions.

For obvious reafons, his Latin pieces, though excellent in their kind, can never ácquire the popularity of the Englifh: Thofe who read with pleafure the Latin claffics, fee their inferiority; to others, they are uninterefting and unintelligible. " The delight which they afford;" to ufe his own words, in criticifing the Latin poetry of Milton, " is rather by the exquifite imitation of the ancient writers, by the purity of the diction, and the harmony of the numbers, than by any power of invention, or vigour of fentiment." This character will generally fuit our modern Latin poetry; for if we except that noble ode of Gray's, written at the Grande Chartreufe, and fome few others, there are not many of the *Poemata Anglorum*, that contain much " power of invention, or vigour of fentiment."

Upon the whole, the various productions of Johnfon fhow a life fpent in ftudy and meditation. It may be fairly allowed, as he ufed to fay of himfelf, that *he has writ-*

ten his share. His oddities and infirmities in common life, will, after a while, be overlooked and forgotten; but his writings will remain a monument of his genius and learning; still more and more studied and admired, while Britons shall continue to be characterized by a love of elegance and sublimity, of good sense and virtue. In the works of Johnson, the reader will find a perpetual source of pleasure and instruction. With due precaution, men may learn to give to their style, elegance, harmony, and precision; they may be taught to think with vigour and perspicuity; and all, by a diligent attention to his writings, may advance in virtue.

The character of Johnson, as given by Mr. Boswell in the conclusion of his work, is delineated with a masterly pencil. The drawing appears to be sufficiently accurate, the light and shade well distributed, and the colouring very little overcharged or heightened; though a favourable likeneſs was perhaps in ſome degree intended, as far as might ſeem conſiſtent with the truth of reſemblance, and no farther.

" His figure was large and well-formed, and his countenance of the caſt of an ancient ſtatue; yet his appearance was rendered ſtrange and ſomewhat uncouth, by convulſive cramps, by the ſcars of that diſtemper which it was once imagined the royal touch could cure, and by a ſlovenly mode of dreſs. He had the uſe only of one eye; yet ſo much does mind govern, and even ſupply the deficiency of organs, that his viſual perceptions, as far as they extended, were uncommonly quick and accurate. So morbid was his temperament, that he never knew the natural joy of a free and vigorous uſe of his limbs: when he walked, it was like the ſtruggling gait of one in fetters; when he rode, he had no command or direction of his horfe, but was carried as if in a balloon. That, with his conftitution and habits of life, he fhould have lived feventy-five years, is a proof that an inherent *vivida vis* is a powerful prefervative of the human frame.

" Man is in general made up of contradictory qualities, and thefe will ever fhow themfelves in ftrange fucceffion, where a confiftency, in appearance at leaft, if not in reality, has not been attained by long habits of philofophical difcipline. In proportion to the native vigour of the mind, the contradictory qualities will be the more prominent, and more difficult to be adjufted; and therefore we are not to wonder, that Johnfon exhibited an eminent example of this remark which I have made upon human nature. At different times he feemed a different man, in fome refpects; not, however, in any great or effential article, upon which he had fully em-

ployed his mind, and fettled certain principles of duty, but only in his manners,
and in difplays of argument and fancy in
his talk. - He was prone to fuperftition, but
not to credulity.   Though his imagination
might incline him to a belief of the marvellous and the myfterious, his vigorous
reafon examined the evidence with jealou-
fy.   He was a fincere and zealous Chriftian, of high church of England and mo-
narchical principles, which he would not
tamely fuffer to be queftioned; and had,
perhaps, at an early period, narrowed his
mind fomewhat too much, both as to religion and politics. His being impreffed with
the danger of extreme latitude in eit'er,
though he was of a very independent fpirit,
occafioned his appearing fomewhat unfavourable to the prevalence of that noble
freedom of fentiment which is the beft poffeffion of man.   Nor can it be denied, that
he had many prejudices; which, however,

frequently fuggefted many of his pointed fayings, that rather fhow a playfulnefs of fancy, than any fettled malignity. He was fteady and inflexible in maintaining the obligations of religion and morality, both from a regard for the order of fociety, and from a veneration for the Great Source of all order; correct, nay ftern in his tafte; hard to pleafe, and eafily offended; impetuous and irritable in his temper, but of a moft humane and benevolent heart, which fhowed itfelf not only in a moft liberal charity, as far as his circumftances would allow, but in a thoufand inftances of active benevolence. He was afflicted with a bodily difeafe which made him reftlefs and fretful, and with a conftitutional melancholy, the clouds of which darkened the brightnefs of his fancy, and gave a gloomy caft to his whole courfe of thinking: we therefore ought not to wonder at his fallies of impatience and paffion at any time, efpe-

cially when provoked by obtrusive ignorance, or presuming petulance ; and allowance must be made for his uttering hasty
and satirical sallies, even against his best
friends. And surely, when it is considered, that " amidst sickness and sorrow,"
he exerted his faculties in so many works
for the benefit of mankind, and particularly that he achieved the great and admirable Dictionary of our language, we must
be astonished at his resolution. The solemn text of " him to whom much is giv-
en, much will be required," seems to have
been ever present to his mind in a rigorous sense, and to have made him dissatisfied
with his labours and acts of goodness; however comparatively great ; so that the un-
avoidable conscioufness of his superiority
was in that respect a cause of disquiet: He
suffered so much from this, and from the
gloom which perpetually haunted him, and
made solitude frightful, that it may be said

of him, " If in this life only he had hope," he was of all men moft miferable." He loved praife when it was brought to him ; but was too proud to feek for it. He was fomewhat fufceptible of flattery. As he was general and unconfined in his ftudies, he cannot be confidered as mafter of any one particular fcience ; but he had accumulated a vaft and various collection of learning and knowledge, which was fo arranged in his mind, as to be ever in readinefs to be brought forth. But his fuperiority over other learned men confifted chiefly in what may be called the art of thinking, the art of ufing his mind ; a certain continual power of feizing the ufeful fubftance of all that he knew, and exhibiting it in a clear and forcible manner ; fo that knowledge which we often fee to be no better than lumber in men of dull underftanding, was in him true, evident, and actual wifdom. His moral precepts are

practical ; for they are drawn from an intimate acquaintance with human nature.
His maxims carry conviction ; for they are
founded on the bafis of common fenfe. His
mind was fo full of imagery, that he might
have been perpetually a poet ; yet it is remarkable, that however rich his profe is in
that refpect, the poetical pieces which he
wrote were in general not fo, but rather
ftrong fentiment and acute obfervation,
conveyed in good verfe, particularly in heroic couplets. Though ufually grave, and
even awful in his deportment, he poffeffed uncommon and peculiar powers of wit
and humour : he frequently indulged himfelf in colloquial pleafantry ; and the hearti-
eft merriment was often enjoyed in his
company ; with this great advantage, that
as it was entirely free from any poifonous
tincture of vice or impiety, it was falutary
to thofe who fhared in it. He had accuftomed himfelf to fuch accuracy in his com-

[263]

men converſation, that he at all times delivered himſelf with a force, choice, and
elegance of expreſſion, the effect of which
was aided by his having a loud voice, and
a ſlow and deliberate utterance. He united a moſt logical head with a moſt fertile
imagination, which gave him an extraordinary advantage in arguing ; for he could
reaſon cloſe or wide, as he ſaw beſt for the
moment. Exulting in his intellectual
ſtrength and dexterity, he could, when he
pleaſed, be the greateſt ſophiſt that ever
contended in the liſts of declamation ; and
from a ſpirit of contradiction, and a delight
in ſhowing his powers, he would often
maintain the wrong ſide with equal warmth
and ingenuity: ſo that when there was an
audience, his real opinions could ſeldom be
gathered from his talk ; though when he
was in company with a ſingle friend, he
would diſcuſs a ſubject with genuine fair-
neſs. But he was too conſcientious to make

R iiij

error permanent and pernicious, by deliberately writing it; and in all his numerous works, he earneftly inculcated what appeared to him to be the truth. His piety was conftant, and was the ruling principle of all his conduct; and the more we confider his character, we fhall be the more difpofed to regard him with admiration and reverence."

His character, as given by Mrs. Piozzi in her " Anecdotes," is drawn with fpirit and propriety, though fomewhat lefs favourably.

" His ftature was remarkably high, and his limbs exceedingly large: his ftrength was more than common, I believe, and his activity had been greater, I have heard, than fuch a form gave one reafon to expect: his features were ftrongly marked, and his countenance particularly rugged; though the original complexion had certainly been fair, a circumftance fomewhat unufual, his fight was near, and otherwife imperfect; yet his eyes, though of a light-gray colour, were fo wild, fo piercing, and at times fo fierce, that fear was, I believe, the firft emotion in the hearts of all his beholders. His mind was fo comprehenfive, that no language but that he ufed could have expreffed its contents; and fo ponderous was his language, that fentiments lefs lofty and lefs folid than his were, would have been encumbered, not adorned by it.

"Mr. Johnfon was not intentionally, however, a pompous converfer: and though he was accufed of ufing big words, as they are called, it was only when little ones could not exprefs his meaning as clearly, or when, perhaps, the elevation of the thought would have been difgraced by a drefs lefs fuperb. He ufed to fay, " that the fize of a man's underftanding might always be juftly meafured by his mirth;" and his own was never contemptible. He would laugh at a

ftroke of genuine humour, or fudden fally
of odd abfurdity, as heartily and freely as I
ever yet faw any man ; and though the jeft
was often fuch as few felt befides himfelf,
yet his laugh was irrefiftible, and was obferved immediately to produce that of the
company, not merely from the notion that
it was proper to laugh when he did, but
purely out of want of power to forbear it.
He was no enemy to fplendour of apparel,
or pomp of equipage. " Life," he would
fay, " is barren enough, furely, with all her
trappings; let us therefore be cautious how
we ftrip her."

" Of Mr. Johnfon's erudition the world
has been the judge; and we who produce
each a fcore of his fayings, as proofs of that
wit which in him was inexhauftible, re-
femble travellers, who, having vifited Delhi
or Golconda, bring home each a handful
of oriental pearl, to evince the riches of
the Great Mogul.

" As his purſe was ever open to alms-
giving, ſo was his heart tender to thoſe who
wanted relief, and his ſoul ſuſceptible of
gratitude, and of every kind impreſſion;
yet, though he had refined his ſenſibility,
he had not endangered his quiet, by encou-
raging in himſelf a ſolicitude about trifles,
which he treated with the contempt they
deſerve.

" Mr. Johnſon had a roughneſs in his
manner, which ſubdued the ſaucy, and
terrified the meek : this was, when I knew
him, the prominent part of a character
which few durſt venture to approach ſo
nearly, and which was for that reaſon in
many reſpects groſsly and frequently miſtaken; and it was, perhaps, peculiar to
him, that the lofty conſcioufneſs of his own
ſuperiority, which animated his looks, and
raiſed his voice in converſation, caſt like-
wiſe an impenetrable veil over him when
he ſaid nothing. His talk, therefore, had

commonly the complexion of arrogance, his filence of fupercilioufnefs. He was, however, feldom inclined to be filent when any moral or literary queftion was ftarted; and it was on fuch occafions that, like the fage in *Raffelas*, he fpoke, and attention watched his lips; he reafoned, and conviction clofed his periods. If poetry was talked of, his quotations were the readieft; and had he not been eminent for more folid and brilliant qualities, mankind would have united to extol his extraordinary memory. His manner of repeating deferves to be defcribed, though, at the fame time, it defeats all power of defcription; but whoever once heard him repeat an ode of Horace, would be long before they could endure to hear it repeated by another.

" His equity in giving the character of living acquaintance, ought not, undoubtedly, to be omitted in his own, whence partiality and prejudice were totally excluded, and truth alone prefided in his tongue; a fteadinefs of conduct the more to be commended, as no man had ftronger likings or averfions. His veracity was, indeed, from the moft trivial to the moft folemn occafions, ftrict, even to feverity; he fcorned to embellifh a ftory with fictitious circumftances, which (he ufed to fay), took off from its real value. " A ftory," fays Johnfon, " fhould be a fpecimen of life and manners; but if the furrounding circumftances are falfe, as it is no more a reprefentation of reality, it is no longer worthy our attention."

" For the reft—That beneficence which, during his life, increafed the comforts of fo many, may, after his death, be, perhaps, ungratefully forgotten; but that piety which dictated the ferious papers in the *Rambler*, will be for ever remembered, for ever, I think, revered. That ample repofitory of religious truth, moral wifdom, and accu-

rate criticifm, breathes, indeed, the genuine emanations of its great author's mind,
expreffed, too, in a ftyle fo natural to him,
and fo much like his common mode of
converfing, that I was myfelf but little a-
ftonifhed, when he told me that he had
fcarcely read over one of thofe inimitable
effays before they went to the prefs.

" I will add one or two peculiarities
more : Though at an immeafurable dif-
tance from content in the contemplation
of his own uncouth form and figure, he did
not like another man much the lefs for being a coxcomb. Though a man of obfcure
birth himfelf, his partiality to people of family was vifible on every occafion ; his zeal
for fubordination warm even to bigotry;
his hatred to innovation, and reverence for
the old feudal times, apparent, whenever
any poffible manner of fhowing them occurred. I have fpoken of his piety, his
charity, and his truth, the enlargement of

his heart, and the delicacy of his fentiments; and when I fearch for fhadow to
my portrait, none can I find but what was
formed by pride, differently modified as different occafions fhowed it; yet never was
pride fo purified as Johnfon's, at once from
meannefs and from vanity. The mind of
this man was, indeed, expanded beyond the
common limits of human nature, and ftor-
ed with fuch variety of knowledge, that I
ufed to think it refembled a royal plea-
fure-ground, where every plant, of every
name and nation, flourifhed in the full perfection of their powers, and where, though
lofty woods and falling cataracts firft caught
the eye, and fixed the earlieft attention of
beholders, yet neither the trim parterre,
nor the pleafing fhrubbery, nor even the
antiquated evergreens, were denied a place
in fome fit corner of the happy valley."

His character, as given by Dr. Towers,
in his " Effay," appears to have been writ-

ten under no impreffions of prepoffeffion or
prejudice, and exhibits a very commend-
able degree of candour, impartiality, and
precifion.

" He poffeffed extraordinary powers of
underftanding, which were much cultivated by ftudy, and ftill more by meditation
and reflection. His memory was remarkably retentive, his imagination uncommonly vigorous, and his judgment keen and pe-
netrating. He had a ftrong fenfe of the
importance of religion ; his piety was fincere, and fometimes ardent ; and his zeal
for the interefts of virtue was often manifefted in his converfation and in his writings. The fame energy which was difplayed in his literary productions, was exhibited alfo in his converfation, which was various, ftriking, and inftructive ; and, perhaps, no man ever equalled him for nervous and pointed repartees.

" The great originality which fometimes appeared in his conceptions, and the perfpicuity and force with which he delivered them, greatly enhanced the value of his converfation; and the remarks that he delivered, received additional weight from the ftrength of his voice, and the folemnity of his manner. He was confcious of his own fuperiority; and when in company with literary men, or with thofe with whom there was any poffibility of rivalfhip or competition, this confcioufnefs was too apparent. With inferiors, and thofe who readily admitted all his claims, he was often mild and agreeable; but to others, fuch was often the arrogance of his manners, that the endurance of it required no ordinary degree of patience. He was very dexterous at argumentation; and when his reafonings were not folid, they were at leaft artful and plaufible. His retorts were fo powerful, that his friends and acquaintance were generally cautious of entering the lifts againft him; and the ready acquiefcence of thofe, with whom he affociated, in his opinions and affertions, probably rendered him more dogmatic than he might otherwife have been. With thofe, however, with whom he lived, and with whom he was familiar, he was fometimes cheerful and fprightly, and fometimes indulged himfelf in fallies of wit and pleafantry. He fpent much of his time, efpecially his latter years, in converfation, and feems to have had fuch an averfion to being left without company, as was fometimes extraordinary in a man poffeffed of fuch intellectual powers, and whofe underftanding had been fo highly cultivated.

" He fometimes difcovered much impetuofity of temper, and was too ready to take offence at others; but when conceffions were made, he was eafily appeafed. For thofe from whom he had received kind-

nefs in the earlier part of his life, he feemed ever to retain a particular regard, and
manifefted much gratitude towards thofe
by whom he had at any time been bene-
fited. He was foon offended with pert-
nefs or ignorance; but he fometimes feemed to be confcious of having anfwered the
queftions of others with too much rough-
nefs, and was then defirous to difcover
more gentlenefs of temper, and to com-
municate information with more fuavity
of manners. When not under the influence of perfonal pique, of pride, or of religious or political prejudices, he feems to
have had great ardour of benevolence; and,
on fome occafions, he gave fignal proofs of
generofity and humanity.

" He was naturally melancholy, and his
views of human life appear to have been
habitually gloomy. This appears from his
Raffelas, and in many paffages of his writings. It was alfo a ftriking part of the cha-

racter of Johnson, that with powers of mind that did honour to human nature, he had weakneſſes and prejudices that ſeemed ſuited only to the loweſt of the ſpecies. His piety was ſtrongly tinctured with ſuperſtition; and we are aſtoniſhed to find the author of the *Rambler* expreſſing ſerious concern, becauſe he had put milk into his tea on a Good-Friday. His cuſtom of praying for the dead, though unſupported by reaſon or by Scripture, was a leſs irrational ſuperſtition. Indeed, one of the great features of Johnſon's character, was a degree of bigotry, both in politics and in religion, which is now ſeldom to be met with in perſons of a cultivated underſtanding. Few other men could have been found in the preſent age, whoſe political bigotry would have led them to ſtyle the celebrated John Hampden " the zealot of rebellion;" and the religious bigotry of the man, who, when at Edinburgh, would not go to hear

Dr. Robertson preach, becaufe he would not be prefent at a Prefbyterian affembly, is not eafily to be paralleled in this age and in this country. His habitual incredulity with refpect to facts, of which there was no reafonable ground for doubt, as ftated by Mrs. Piozzi, and which was remarked by Hogarth, was alfo a fingular trait in his character, and efpecially when contrary to his fuperftitious credulity on other occafions. To the clofe of life he was not only occupied in forming fchemes of religious reformation ; but, even to a very late period of it, he feems to have been folicitous to apply himfelf to ftudy with renewed diligence and vigour. It is remarkable, that in his fixty-fourth year, he attempted to learn the low Dutch language ; and in his fixty-feventh year he made a refolution to apply himfelf vigoroufly to ftudy, particularly the Greek and Italian tongues.

" The faults and the foibles of Johnfon, whatever they were, are now defcended with him to the grave; but his virtues fhould be the object of our imitation. His works, with all their defects, are a moft valuable and important acceffion to the literature of England. His political writings will probably be little read on any other account, than for the dignity and energy of his ftyle; but his Dictionary, his Moral Effays, and his productions in polite literature, will convey ufeful inftruction and elegant entertainment, as long as the language in which they are written fhall be underftood, and give him a juft claim to a diftinguifhed rank among the beft and ableft writers that England has produced."

The eftimate of his literary character given by Mr. Murphy in his " Effay," is, with a very few exceptions, fair, candid, and juft. He fometimes admits his errors, and fometimes endeavours to apologize for them. His comparison between Johnson and Addison is excellent; and, though long, is of too much value to be withheld.

"Like Milton and Addison, Dr. Johnson seems to have been fond of his Latin poetry. Those compositions show that he was an early scholar; but his verses have not the graceful ease that gave so much suavity to the poems of Addison. The translation of the Messiah labours under two disadvantages; it is first to be compared with Pope's inimitable performance, and afterwards with the Pollio of Virgil. It may appear trifling to remark, that he has made the letter *o*, in the word *Virgo*, long and short in the same line ; *Virgo, Virgo parit*. But the translation has great merit, and some admirable lines. In the *Odes* there is a sweet flexibility, particularly *To his Worthy Friend Dr. Laurence*, on *Himself at the Theatre*, March 8. 1771, the *Ode* in the Ifle of Sky, and that to *Mrs. Thrale*, from the fame place.

" His Englifh poetry is fuch as leaves room to think, if he had devoted himfelf to the Mufes, that he would have been the rival of Pope. His firft production in this kind was *London*, a poem, in imitation of the third fatire of Juvenal. The vices of the metropolis are placed in the room of ancient manners. The author had heated his mind with the ardour of Juvenal; and, having the fkill to polifh his numbers, he became a fharp accufer of the times. The *Vanity of Human Wifhes* is an imitation of the tenth fatire of the fame author. Though it is tranflated by Dryden, Johnfon's imitation approaches neareft to the fpirit of the original.

" What Johnfon has faid of the Tragedy of Cato, may be applied to *Irene:* " It is rather a poem in dialogue than a drama; rather a fucceffion of juft fentiments in ele-

gant language, than a reprefentation of natural affections. Nothing excites or af-
fuages emotion. The events are expected
without folicitude, and are remembered
without joy or forrow. Of the agents we
have no care; we confider not what they
are doing, nor what they are fuffering;
we wifh only to know what they have to
fay. It is unaffecting elegance, and chill
philofophy.

" The prologue to *Irene* is written with
elegance, and, in a peculiar ftrain, fhows
the literary pride and lofty fpirit of the
author. The epilogue, we are told in a late
publication, was written by Sir William
Yonge. This is a new difcovery, but by
no means probable. When the append-
ages to a dramatic performance are not affigned to a friend, or an unknown hand, or
a perfon of fafhion, they are always fuppofed to be written by the author of the
play. It is to be wifhed, however, that the

epilogue in question could be transferred to any other writer. It is the worst *Jeu d' Esprit* that ever fell from Johnson's pen.

" Of his *Miscellaneous Tracts* and *Philological Dissertations*, it will suffice to say, they are the productions of a man who never wanted decorations of language, and always taught his reader to think. The *Life of the late King of Prussia*, as far as it extends, is a model of the biographical style. The *review* of the " Origin of Evil," was, perhaps, written with asperity; but the angry epitaph, which it provoked from Soame Jenyns, was an ill-timed resentment, unworthy of the genius of that amiable author.

" The *Rambler* may be considered as Johnson's great work. It was the basis of that high reputation which went on increasing to the end of his days. In this collection, Johnson is the great moral teacher of his countrymen; his essays form a body of ethics; the observations on life and man-

ners are acute and inftructive; and the papers, profeffedly critical, ferve to promote
the caufe of literature. It muft, however,
be acknowledged, that a fettled gloom hangs
over the author's mind; and all the effays,
except eight or ten, coming from the fame
fountain-head, no wonder that they have
the racinefs of the foil from which they
fprung. Of this uniformity Johnfon was
fenfible. He ufed to fay, that if he had
joined a friend or two, who would have
been able to intermix papers of a fprightly turn, the collection would have been
more mifcellaneous, and by confequence,
more agreeable to the generality of readers.

" It is remarkable that the pomp of diction, which has been objected to Johnfon,
was firft affumed in the *Rambler*. His
Dictionary was going on at the fame time;
and in the courfe of that work, as he grew
familiar with technical and fcholaftic words,
he thought that the bulk of his readers

were equally learned, or at leaft would admire the fplendour and dignity of the ftyle.
And yet it is well known, that he praifed
in Cowley the eafe and unaffected ftructure of the fentences. Cowley may be placed at the head of thofe who cultivated a
clear and natural ftyle. Dryden, Tillotfon,
and Sir William Temple followed. Addifon, Swift, and Pope, with more correctnefs, carried our language well nigh to perfection. Of Addifon, Johnfon was ufed
to fay, he is the Raphael of effay writers.
How he differed fo widely from fuch elegant models, is a problem not to be folved,
unlefs it be true that he took an early tincture from the writers of the laft century,
particularly Sir Thomas Brown.—Hence
the peculiarities of his ftyle, new combina-
tions, fentences of an unufual ftructure, and
words derived from the learned languages.
His own account of the matter is, " when
common words were lefs pleafing to the ear,

or lefs diftinct in their fignification, I fa-
miliarized the terms of philofophy, by applying them to popular ideas." But he
forgot the obfervation of Dryden : *If too
many foreign words are poured in upon us, it
looks as if they were defigned, not to affift the
natives, but to conquer them.* There is, it
muft be admitted, a fwell of language, often out of all proportion to the fentiment ;
but there is, in general, a fulnefs of mind,
and the thought feems to expand with the
found of the words. Determined to dif-
card colloquial barbarifms and licentious
idioms, he forgot the elegant fimplicity that
diftinguifhes the writings of Addifon. He
had what Locke calls a round-about view
of his fubject ; and, though he was never
tainted like many modern wits, with the
ambition of fhining in the paradox, he may
be fairly called an *original thinker.* His
reading was extenfive. He treafured in his
mind whatever was worthy of notice ; but

hè added to it from his own meditation. He collected, *quæ reconderet, actaque promeret.* Addifon was not fo profound a thinker. He was born to write, converfe, and live with eafe; and he found an early patron in Lord Somers. He depended, however, more upon a fine tafte, than the vigour of his mind. His Latin poetry fhows, that he relifhed, with a juft felection, all the refined and delicate beauties of the Roman claffics; and when he cultivated his native language, no wonder that he formed that graceful ftyle, which has been fo juftly admired; fimple, yet elegant; adorned, yet never over-wrought; rich in illufion, yet pure and perfpicuous; correct, without labour; and, though fometimes deficient in ftrength, yet always mufical. His effays, in general, are on the furface of life; if ever original, it was in pieces of humour. Sir Roger de Coverly, and the Tory Fox-hunter, need not be mentioned,

Johnson had a fund of humour, but he did not know it;—nor was he willing to descend to the familiar idiom, and the variety of diction which that mode of compofition required. The letter, in the *Rambler*, No. 12. from a young girl that wants a place, will illuftrate this obfervation. Addifon poffeffed an unclouded imagination, alive to the firft objects of nature and of art. He reaches the fublime without any apparent effort. When he tells us, " if we confider the fixed ftars as fo many oceans of flame, that are each of them attended with a different fet of planets; if we ftill difcover new firmaments and new lights, that are funk further in thofe unfathomable depths of æther, we are loft in a labyrinth of funs and worlds, and confounded with the magnificence and immenfity of nature." The eafe with which this paffage rifes to an unaffected grandeur, is the fecret charm that captivates the reader. Johnfon is always lofty ; he feems to ufe Dryden's phrafe, to be o'er inform'd with meaning, and his words do not appear to himfelf adequate to his conception. He moves in ftate, and his periods are always harmonious. His *Oriental Tales* are in the true ftyle of eaftern magnificence, and yet none of them are fo much admired as the vifions of Mirza. In matters of criticifm, Johnfon is never the echo of preceding writers. He thinks and decides for himfelf. If we except the Effays on the pleafures of imagination, Addifon cannot be called a philofophical critic. His moral Effays are beautiful ; but in that province nothing can exceed the *Rambler ;* though Johnfon ufed to fay, that the effay on the burdens of mankind (in the Spectator, No. 558) was the moft exquifite he had ever read. Talking of himfelf, Johnfon faid, " Topham Beauclerk has wit, and every thing comes from him with eafe; but when I fay a good thing, I feem to labour." When we compare him with Addifon, the contraft is ftill ftronger. Addifon lends grace and ornament to truth; Johnfon gives it force and energy. Addifon makes virtue amiable; Johnfon reprefents it as an awful duty. Addifon infinuates himfelf with an air of modefty; Johnfon commands like a dictator; but a dictator in his fplendid robes, not labouring at his plough. Addifon is the Jupiter of Virgil, with placid ferenity talking to Venus:

" Vultu, quo cœlum tempeftatefque ferenat."

Johnfon is *Jupiter tonans:* he darts his lightning, and rolls his thunder, in the caufe of virtue and piety. The language feems to fall fhort of his ideas; he pours along, familiarifing the terms of philofophy with bold inverfions and fonorous periods; but we may apply to him what

T

Pope has said of Homer: " It is the sentiment
that swells and fills out the diction, which
rises with it, and forms itself about it ;
like glass in the furnace, which grows to
a greater magnitude, as the breath within
is more powerful, and the heat more intense."

" The essays written by Johnson in the
" Adventurer," may be called a continu-
ation of the *Rambler*. The *Idler*, in order
to be consistent with the assumed character, is written with abated vigour, in a style
of ease and unlaboured elegance. It is
the Odyssey after the Iliad. Intense thinking would not become the *Idler*. The
first number presents a well-drawn portrait of an idler ; and from that character
no deviation could be made. Accordingly Johnson forgets his austere manner, and
plays us into sense. He still continues his
lectures on human life ; but he adverts to
common occurrences, and is often content

with the topic of the day. This account
of the *Idler* may be clofed, after obferving,
that the author's mother being buried on
the 23d of January 1759, there is an admirable paper, occafioned by that event,
on Saturday the 27th of the fame month,
No. 41. The reader, if he pleafes, may
compare it with another fine paper in the
Rambler, No. 41, on the conviction that
rufhes on the mind at the bed of a dying
friend.

" *Raffelas*," fays Sir John Hawkins, " is
a fpecimen of our language fcarcely to be
paralleled ; it is written in a ftyle refined
to a degree of *immaculate purity*, and difplays the whole force of *turgid* eloquence."
One cannot but fmile at this encomium.
Raffelas is undoubtedly both elegant and
fublime. It is a view of human life, difplayed, it muft be owned, in gloomy colours.
The author's natural melancholy, depreffed at the time by the approaching diffolu-

tion of his mother, darkened the picture.
A tale that should keep curiosity awake
by the artifice of unexpected incidents,
was not the design of a mind pregnant
with better things. He who reads the
heads of the chapters, will find that it is
not a course of adventures that invites
him forward, but a discussion of interest-
ing questions; Reflections on Human
Life; the History of Imlac, the Man of
Learning; a Dissertation upon Poetry;
the Character of a Wise and Happy Man,
who discourses with energy on the government of the passions, and on a sudden,
when death deprives him of his daughter,
forgets all his maxims of wisdom, and the
eloquence that adorned them, yielding to
the stroke of affliction with all the vehe-
mence of the bitterest anguish. It is by
pictures of life, and profound moral reflection, that expectation is engaged and
gratified throughout the work. The His-

tory of the Mad Aftronomer, who imagines that for five years he poffeffed the regulation of the weather, and that the fun paffed from tropic to tropic by his direction, reprefents, in ftricting colours, the fad effects of a diftempered imagination. It becomes the more affecting, when we recollect that it proceeds from one who lived in fear of the fame dreadful vifitation; from one, who fays emphatically, " Of the uncertainties in our prefent ftate, the moft dreadful and alarming is the uncertain continuance of reafon." The inquiry into the caufe of madnefs, and the dangerous prevalence of imagination, till in time fome particular train of ideas fixes the attention, and the mind recurs conftantly to the favourite conception, is carried on in a ftrain of acute obfervation; but it leaves us room to think that the author was tranfcribing from his own apprehenfions. The difcourfe on the nature of the foul gives us all that philofophy knows ; not without a tincture of fuperftition. It is remarkable that the vanity of human purfuits was, about the fame time, the fubject that employed both Johnfon and Voltaire ; but *Candide* is the work of a lively imagination, and Raffelas, with all its fplendour of eloquence; exhibits a gloomy picture.

" The *Dictionary*, though in fome inftances abufe has been loud, and in others malice has endeavoured to undetermine its fame, ftill remains the *Mount Atlas* of Englifh literature.

> Though ftorms and tempefts thunder on its brow,
> And oceans break their billows at its feet,
> It ftands unmov'd, and glories in its height.

" That Johnfon was eminently qualified for the office of a commentator on *Shakfpeare*, no man can doubt ; but it was an office which he never cordially embraced. The public expected more than he had diligence to perform ; and yet his edition has been the ground on which every fub-fequent commentator has chofe to build. The general obfervations at the end of the feveral plays, with great elegance and pre-cifion, give a fummary view of each drama. The preface is a tract of great eru-dition and philofophical criticifm.

" Johnfon's *political pamphlets*, whatever was his motive for writing them, whether gratitude for his penfion, or the folicitation of men in power, did not fupport the caufe for which they were undertaken. They are written in a ftyle truly harmonious, and with his ufual dignity of language. When it is faid that he advanced pofitions repugnant to *the common rights of mankind*, the virulence of party may be fufpected. It is, perhaps, true, that in the clamour raifed throughout the kingdom, Johnfon over-heated his mind ; but he was a friend to the rights of man, and he was

greatly fuperior to the littlenefs of fpirit
that might incline him to advance what
he did not think and firmly believe.

" The account of his *Journey to the Hebrides* or Weftern Ifles of Scotland, is a
model for fuch as fhall hereafter relate
their travels. The author did not vifit
that part of the world in the character of
an antiquary, to amufe us with wonders
taken from the dark and fabulous ages;
nor as a mathematician, to meafure a degree, and fettle the longitude and latitude
of the feveral iflands. Thofe who expected fuch information, expected what was
never intended.

In every work regard the writer's end.

Johnfon went to fee men and manners,
modes of life, and the progrefs of civiliza-
tion. His remarks are fo artfully blended
with the rapidity and elegance of his narrative, that the reader is inclined to wifh,

as Johnſon did with regard to Gray, that *to travel, and to tell his travels, had been more of his employment.*

" We come now to the *Lives of the Poets,* a work undertaken at the age of ſeventy, yet the moſt brilliant, and certainly the moſt popular of all our author's writings. For this performance he needed little preparation. Attentive always to the hiſtory of letters, and by his own natural bias fond of biography, he was the more willing to embrace the propoſition of the bookſellers. He was verſed in the whole body of the Engliſh poetry, and his rules of criticiſm were ſettled with preciſion. The facts are related upon the beſt intelligence, and the beſt vouchers that could be gleaned, after a great lapſe of time. Probability was to be inferred from ſuch materials as could be procured, and no man better underſtood the nature of hiſtorical evidence than Johnſon; no man was more religiously an obferver of truth. If his hiftory is any where defective, it muft be imputed to the want of better information, and the errors of uncertain tradition.

Ad nos vix tenuis famæ prelabitur aura.

" If the ftrictures on the works of the various authors are not always fatisfactory, and if erroneous criticifm may fometimes be fufpected, who can hope, that, in matters of tafte, all fhall agree? The inftances in which the public mind has differed from the pofitions advanced by the author, are few in number. It has been faid, that juftice has not been done to Swift; that Gay and Prior are undervalued; and that Gray has been harfhly treated. This charge, perhaps, ought not to be difputed. Johnfon, it is well known, had conceived a prejudice againft Swift. His friends trembled for him when he was writing that life, but were pleafed, at laft, to fee it executed with temper and moderation. As to Prior, it is probable that he gave his real opinion; but an opinion that will not be adopted by men of lively fancy. With regard to Gray, when he condemns the apoftrophe, in which Father Thames is defired to tell who drives the hoop or toffes the ball, and then adds, that Father Thames had no better means of knowing than himfelf; when he compares the abrupt beginning of the firft ftanza of the " Bard" to the ballad of " Johnny Armftrong," " *Is there ever a man in all Scotland;*" there are, perhaps, few friends of Johnfon, who would not wifh to blot out both the paffages."

The following quotation from Horace is given by Mr. Murphy, as containing Johnfon's picture in miniature.

" Iracundior eft paulo minus aptus acutis
Naribus horum hominum, rideri poffit, eo quid

Rufticius tonfo toga defluit, et male laxus
In pede calceus hæret.   At eft bonus, ut melior vir
Non alius quifquam; at tibi amicus, at ingenium ingens
Inculto latet hoc fub corpore."————

His moral and literary character has been delineated by Mifs Seward the poetefs of Litchfield, in the " European Magazine" for 1785, with equal accuracy of difcrimination and ftrength of colouring.

" Dr. Johnfon's learning and knowledge were deep and univerfal. His conception was fo clear, and his intellectual ftores were marfhalled with fuch precifion, that his ftyle in common converfation equalled that of his moral effays. Whatever charge of pedantic ftiffnefs may have been brought againft thofe effays, by prejudice, or by perfonal refentment, they are certainly not lefs fuperior to all other Englifh compofitions of that fort, in the happy fertility and efflorefcence of imagination, harmony of period, and luminous arrangement of ideas, than they are in ftrength of expreffion, and force of argument. His Latinifms, for which he has been much cenfured, have extended the limits of our native dialect, befides enriching its founds with that fonorous fweetnefs, which the intermixture of words from a more har- monious language muft neceffarily pro- duce; I mean in general, for it cannot be denied that they fometimes deform the Johnfonian page, though they much of- tener adorn it. His *London* is a very bril- liant and nervous fatiric poem, and his *Vanity of Human Wifhes* appears to me a much finer fatire than the beft of Pope's. Per- haps its poetic beauty is not excelled by any compofition in heroic rhyme which this country can boaft, rich as fhe is in that fpecies of writing. As a moralift, Dr. Johnfon was refpectable, fplendid, fu- blime; but as a critic, the faults of his difpofition have difgraced much of his fine writings with frequent paradox, unprin-cipled mifreprefentation, mean and need-lefs expofure of bodily infirmities (as in the life of Pope), irreconcileable contra-dictions, and with decifions of the laft ab-furdity. Dr. Johnfon had ftrong affec-tions where literary envy did not interfere; but that envy was of fuch deadly potency, as to load his converfation, as it has loaded his biographic works, with the rancour of party violence, with national averfion, bitter farcafm, and unchriftian-like invective. It is in vain to defcant upon the improbability that Dr. Johnfon, under the confcioufnefs of abilities fo great, and of a fame fo extenfive, fhould envy any man, fince it is more than im-probable, it is wholly impoffible, that an imagination fo fublime, and a judgment fo correct, on all abftract fubjects, fhould decide as he has decided upon the works of *fome* who were at leaft his equals, and upon *one* who is yet greater than himfelf. Dr. Johnfon was a furious Jacobite, while one hope for the Stuart line remained ; and his politics, always leaning towards defpotifm, were inimical to liberty, and the natural rights of mankind. He was punctual in his devotions ; but his religious faith had much more of bigot-fiercenefs than of that gentlenefs which the gofpel inculcates. To thofe who had never entered the literary confines, or, entering them, had paid him the tribute of unbounded praife and total fubjection, he was an affectionate and generous friend, foothing in his behaviour to them, and active in promoting their domeftic comforts ; though, in fome fpleenful moments, he could not help fpeaking difrefpectfully both of their mental powers and of their virtues. His pride was infinite; yet, amidft all the overbearing arrogance it produced, his heart melted at the fight or at the reprefentation of difeafe and poverty; and, in the hours of affluence, his purfe was ever open to relieve them. In feveral inftances, his affections feemed unaccountably engaged by people of whofe difpofition and abilities he fcrupled not to fpeak contemptuoufly at all times, and in all humours. To fuch he often devoted, and efpecially of late years, a large portion of that time which might naturally be fuppofed to have been precious to him, who fo well knew how to employ it. When his attention was called to modern writings, particularly if they were celebrated, and not written by any of his " little fenate," he generally liftened with angry impatience. " No, Sir, I fhall not read the book." was his common reply. He turned from the compofitions of rifing genius with a vifible horror, which too plainly proved, that envy was the bofom ferpent of this literary defpot, whofe life had been unpolluted by licentious crimes,

and who had some great and noble qualities, accompanying a stupendous reach of
understanding."

His character, as a poetical biographer,
has been given by his townsman Dr.
Newton, in his posthumous work, not
perhaps with his powers, but with his de-
cision and severity of censure.

" Dr. Johnson's *Lives of the Poets* afford
much amusement, but candour was hurt and
offended at the malevolence that prepon-
derated in every part. Never was any biographer more sparing of his praises, or more
abundant in his censures. He delights
more in exposing blemishes, than in re-
commending beauties; slightly passes over
excellencies; enlarges upon imperfections;
and, not content with his own severe reflections, revives old scandal, and produces
large quotations from the long-forgotten
works of former critics. The panegyrist of
Savage in his youth, may, in his old age,

become the fatirift of the moft favoured authors, his encomium as unjuft and unde-ferved as his cenfures."

The teftimony of the claffical editor of Milton may be compared with the eu-logy pronounced by Dr. Parr, the learned and eloquent editor of " Bellendenus," in his edition of " Tracts by Warburton and a Warburtonian."

" Of literary merit, Johnfon, as we all know, was a fagacious but a moft fevere judge. Such was his difcernment, that he pierced into the moft fecret fprings of hu-man actions; and fuch was his integrity, that he always weighed the moral charac-ters of his fellow creatures in " the balance of the fanctuary."

His peculiarities and foibles are painted in ftrong colours by Mr. Courtenay, in his " Poetical Review ;" but, in return, his vir-tues and abilities are candidly acknowledg-ed, and placed in their proper light. Having alternately commended his merits, and censured his faults, he sums up the whole in the following lines, which strongly mark the character of his work.

"Thus sings the muse, to Johnson's mem'ry just,
And scatters praise and censure o'er his dust;
For, through each chequer'd scene a contrast ran,
Too sad a proof, how great, how weak is man!
Though o'er his passions conscience held the rein,
He shook at dismal phantoms of the brain;
A boundless faith that noble mind debas'd,
By piercing wit, energic reason grac'd:
Ev'n shades like these, to brilliancy allied,
May comfort fools, and curb the sage's pride;
Yet learning's sons, who o'er his foibles mourn,
To latest time shall fondly view his urn;
And, wond'ring, praise, to human frailties blind,
Talents and virtues of the brightest kind.
The sculptur'd trophy and imperial bust,
That proudly rise around his hallow'd dust,
Shall mould'ring fall, by time's slow hand decay'd;
But the bright meed of virtue ne'er shall fade.
Exulting genius stamps his sacred name,
Enroll'd for ever in the dome of fame."

FINIS.

www.ingramcontent.com/pod-product-compliance
Lightning Source LLC
Chambersburg PA
CBHW031044120726
47905CB00007B/2306